# Operation Tomcat

# Operation Camilla

TABITHA ORMISTON-SMITH

http://paradoxbooktrailerproductions.blogspot.com.au

# DEDICATION

For Emily and Ferret.

# ⍏ACKNOWLEDGMENTS⍒

Thank you:

To my wonderful cover designer and friend, Patti Roberts. What a journey it has been. Patti, I value our friendship more than I can say.

To my friend and fellow author, Georgie Ramsey. Thank you for convincing me that Operation Tomcat should be the start of a series. Thank you for being my beta reader. Thank you for your friendship.

To my husband Robert. Thank you for always being there for me. Thank you for being my rock.

And to my precious ones, Emily and Ferret. You keep me sane.

# CONTENTS

# Operation Tomcat

# ℰℴOPERATION TOMCATℭℬ

Tammy staggered up the last few steps and dumped the bags, just as one broke. A can of soup bounced off her foot and smashed a pane in the glass door. Wonderful. The perfect finish to a perfect day.

She fumbled for her keys and after several tries managed to insert the right one. Stepping carefully around the broken glass, she fought an overwhelming urge to howl with grief, rage and despair. The house was a dump, an awful, frightful, cringeworthy dump. Even a full week of scrubbing everything and reducing her French manicure to jagged stumps hadn't done much to alleviate its essential nastiness.

Still, Tammy reflected as she arranged her groceries in the newly scrubbed kitchen cupboards, the house had one undeniable virtue, and that was that she could afford it. Just. Providing nothing went wrong with the car. By the time the lawyers had been paid, there had been only a pitiful remnant of their once healthy bank balance. Enough to buy this shitty house, in this shitty one-horse town, and start over.

It had been easier for Neville. He had just moved into officers' quarters at the base. A nice little bachelor apartment, with an endless supply of nubile young ensigns. It was alright for him, the cheating fucker. While she, Tammy, faithful wife of four and a half years, was reduced to squatting in this – well, whatever it was. The estate agent had called it a 'renovator's delight'. Pretentious fucker with his pointy shoes. House of Horrors was more like it. Still, at least she'd been able to move in right away, despite the settlement funds still not having come through from the lawyer. She'd negotiated a short-term rental agreement. The vendor had been happy enough to let her move in, pending settlement, for a small weekly rent. The house was so trashed she'd been able to get away without having to pay a bond. Just as well, because by the time she'd paid the removal guys, there was just about enough left in her account to buy a week's groceries and a king-sized bottle of Domestos.

Tammy cheered up slightly as she realised that, because contracts had already been signed for her purchase of the house, the vendor would be responsible, as landlord, for replacing the broken pane in the door. She'd go and see him about it tomorrow. First thing tomorrow. Right now, she needed tea. And then more tea. And ice on her foot. Bloody plastic bags. Serve her right, she supposed, for forgetting the green bags again.

She was pouring her second cup of tea when it hit her. There she was relaxing, after a fashion anyway, thinking about which of the stack of frozen meals-for-one she'd bung in the microwave and looking forward to a hot shower and an early night, and there was a fanging great hole in the bloody front door. She'd be murdered in her bed like as not, in this awful neighbourhood. You could reach through a broken pane and undo the Yale lock. She'd seen it often enough in her student days, people in the flats had always been coming home drunk and losing their keys, and they'd break one pane and get in. Chucking the icepack she'd improvised from the surviving supermarket bag into the sink, she grabbed the dustpan from its niche above the fridge and went to survey the damage.

Thank God she'd pulled up that awful seagrass matting, she thought as she swept slivers of glass from the bare floorboards. That would have been a real disaster, with bits of glass sticking in between all the gaps. She'd planned to leave it at first, until she could afford carpet or to get the floors done up, but it had smelt of piss, so she'd hauled it all out for the hard waste collection. It was still sitting in a sodden pile on the nature strip, making its unique contribution to the street's general air of depravity.

The broken pane was right at the bottom. Checking that her keys were in her jeans pocket, Tammy closed the door and knelt gingerly on the porch floor (the doormat had gone along with the seagrass matting) and reached through the hole, swearing as a jagged bit of glass still stuck to the frame caught on her sleeve. She couldn't reach anywhere near the doorknob. Thank God. At least she'd be safe overnight.

She was just about to withdraw (very slowly and carefully, because of the sharp edges) when she heard footsteps behind her, and a light, clear voice said 'Hello, there!' in what were certainly tones of amusement.

'I just got home and saw you seemed to be having some kind of problem,' the voice went on, in accents of pure North Shore. 'Can I do anything? Do you need a doctor?'

Frozen on her knees, bum in the air, Tammy wished for death, or the ground to swallow her up, or to have been born in Africa. Anything, really. She tugged sharply and got her arm out of the hole, tearing a big rip in her last clean shirt. She staggered to her feet.

The stranger was a tall, blonde woman about Tammy's age. She looked like an advertisement. She was the kind of woman you saw in a full-length photo in Vogue, with a leopard on a chain, advertising a luxury car, or a solid gold Rolex, or something. Something Tammy couldn't afford. Not that she could afford Vogue now.

'I'm fine,' she muttered, her face burning. Great, as usual she was turning red. 'I was just, um, testing the door.'

'And did it pass?'

'I, um, see the pane's broken, and I was testing to see if a person could get in that way, see, just in case...'

'I saw you moving in on Saturday, but I thought you might not be quite ready for visitors just at first. It's so difficult moving, isn't it? I'm Vanessa Carlson, by the way. That's my house, just opposite.'

Tammy looked across to where a floodlit McMansion sat in solitary splendour, sticking up above the more or less general depravity of the rest of the street. There was what looked like a late-model Porsche in the driveway. The whole affair looked like a wedding cake in the middle of a garbage tip. Tammy ground her teeth.

'Um, Tammy Norman. I just moved in... oh, yeah, you know that.' Like a drowning man going down for the third time, Tammy snatched at normality. 'Um, would you like to come in? I was just putting the kettle on.'

'Sure, why not?'

Tammy only dropped the keys twice getting the door open, which, she thought bitterly, was probably some kind of record for her. Vanessa Carlson stepped confidently across the threshold, already chattering away. 'I just love what you've done with the...' she trailed into silence as she took in Tammy's front room, almost completely empty and still smelling damply of tea tree oil.

Insincere bitch, thought Tammy. That stopped her stock phrase in its tracks. She sniffed, and felt marginally better.

'I've been mainly just cleaning and scrubbing so far. It was a bit of a mess,' she said as she led the way to the kitchen.

'Oh, I know! I mean, I can imagine! After the trouble.'

'Trouble?'

'Oh, didn't you know? The people who lived here before went crazy, they must have had a bad lot of drugs or something, they were taken away by the police in the end. Such a relief, you know? All that heavy metal music at all hours of the night. I expect they're in rehab somewhere. Or prison, or something.' She settled herself at the kitchen table, looking surprisingly comfortable in the shabby little kitchen. At least it was clean, Tammy comforted herself. She'd stake her life there was no cleaner kitchen in the whole of Australia. The smell of Domestos and tea tree oil would air out. One day.

'So what made you choose Yarrangong? You're not local, are you?'

'No, I'm from Melbourne. My husband – ex-husband, was in the Navy down there. We, I mean I, just wanted to get right away after the divorce, a totally new place, you know? And Yarrangong, well, I thought it would be nice to get somewhere warmer, I looked all round this part of the country...' What the hell, Tammy thought, there was no use pretending. 'This was actually the only house I found that I could afford. There wasn't much left after...'

'After the divorce. I know what it's like. Those lawyers certainly know how to charge, don't they?' Vanessa's tone warmed in sympathy, and Tammy found herself liking the woman a little bit, in spite of her annoying perfection.

'You're not wrong. What about you, are you married?' She had to be, Tammy thought. A yuppie husband, probably a family lawyer, and 2.4 perfect blond children. For sure.

'Yes, my husband, Mario, is away on business.'

'That's a bummer. Will he be gone long?'

Vanessa sighed. 'Could be, it seems to be taking a while this time. Probably another year, we think.'

'A year! Holy shit! You must miss him.' And worry what he's up to, Tammy thought bitterly, if he was anything like bloody Neville.

Vanessa sighed again, a long, melodramatic production that somehow, Tammy thought, seemed a bit overdone, a little... deliberate.

'I do, I do miss him terribly, but it can't be helped. So, what are you planning with this house? You're renovating, of course?'

'Yeah, well it'll be a long business. I pretty well spent everything I had to buy it, so I guess I'll be just doing it a bit at a time as I can afford things.'

'And have you found a job yet?' Smug bitch. She probably hadn't worked a day in her life. Tammy's face burned with shame.

'Sort of, just at Safeway. Just until things...' she trailed off miserably. It wasn't that she was a snob, but just the thought of the checkout waiting for her on Monday brought back the humiliation she'd felt at the dole office. An honours degree in Fine Arts evidently wasn't as good as a typing certificate, and she'd been made to feel like some kind of selfish parasite for having it. It certainly didn't count as a qualification, the man at the counter had sneered. Now if she'd had a certificate in Food Handling, or Mixology (whatever the hell that was, Tammy thought in irritation). The man had rung up Safeway for her on the spot. 'No skills,' he had said, 'but you can train her on the job.'

Vanessa Carlson was now holding forth about her own job teaching Home Economics at all three of the town's high schools, in between dropping the names of various television celebrities. Her husband must be in the entertainment business, Tammy thought. She certainly didn't meet all those glamorous types teaching Home Ec here in Yarrangong. It was a nice enough town in its way, but with a population of only sixty thousand, it was hardly the mecca of Show Biz.

From her own job, Vanessa moved smoothly into Tammy's situation. 'I'd fix that door myself if I were you. Fred Steiner's too lazy to get out of his own way. He wouldn't get out of his own way if his arse was on fire. Have you seen his house? It's the one three doors down, with all the dead cars in the front yard. Honestly, I don't know why the council don't do something. It's a health hazard.'

***

The cat was small, neat and perfect, with a ridiculously long tail. He stepped fastidiously through the broken pane, shaking his hind feet after him, and strolled across the room.

Tammy, who had been staring vacantly into space, pretending to be planning a colour scheme for her sitting room, but actually listening to the echoing silence and feeling sorry for herself, looked up at the movement and froze, her breath catching in delight. She loved cats, and had been planning to adopt one as soon as she was settled with money coming in. She hardly dared to breathe as the cat jumped onto her lap, knocking several colour charts to the floor. She stroked him tentatively, eliciting a loud, rattling purr.

The cat was the traditional kind, Tammy's favourite: black, with white paws and a white shirt front. A massive diamond collar encircled his neck.

He must belong to Vanessa, Tammy decided. Only one house in the street was ostentatious enough to have a diamond collar on the cat. She turned the collar round, but there were no identification tags. Yes, it had to be Vanessa. Spend money on something for show, and completely ignore the one sensible reason for putting a collar on a cat. She edged two fingers inside the collar. A bit snug, but not impossibly tight.

'So, what's your name, fluffball? Hmm? Are you hungry?'

The cat responded by purring even more loudly and kneading Tammy's leg with sharp little claws.

'What's your name, sweetheart? Are you hungry? Would you like some milk?'

The cat jumped off Tammy's lap and ran into the kitchen. He seemed to know where everything was, Tammy thought as she followed him. He sat expectantly in front of the refrigerator, and had to be nudged aside to allow the door to open. Tammy poured him a careful amount of milk in a saucer and set it on the scrubbed floor. He stood on the edge, tipping the milk all over the floor, sniffed at the resultant puddle, shook his feet and jumped up onto the kitchen table.

She ought to ring up Vanessa and let her know

her cat was here, she knew. But what could it hurt, just for this evening, to pretend? Just for a few hours, to have someone else alive in the place. Besides, she didn't know Vanessa's phone number, she told herself. Tammy wasn't taking well to solitary life. On the bases, there'd always been the other Navy wives, and although they'd moved around quite a lot, there had always been new friends to take the place of the old. Not a very satisfying way to live long term, she'd often thought; there had never been any sense of permanence or stability, but there had always been company, and Tammy found the silence of the empty house daunting. When you lived completely alone, the emptiness of the house was somehow different from the emptiness of a house you shared with someone else who was absent. It echoed more, or something.

Having successively declined salami, cheese, the one small steak Tammy had bought to be saved as a treat for herself after her first day at work, and a can of tuna, the cat leapt off the table, plopping to the floor right in the middle of the spilled milk, and strolled back into the sitting room, a trail of milky paw prints marking his progress. He settled into the chair Tammy had vacated, stamped round and round several dozen times, curled up with his tail over his nose, and appeared to go fast asleep.

Tammy sighed and put the now finely chopped steak back in the refrigerator. She could make a stirfry, she supposed, instead of grilling it. She certainly couldn't afford to waste it. It was going to be touch and go till her first paycheck as it was.

After cleaning up the spilt milk and rejected food offerings, Tammy picked up the scattered colour charts, stretched herself on the sofa and returned to her deliberations. She couldn't decide between mushroom, pale yellow and peach. It definitely had to be a warm colour, she decided, shuddering at the horridly vivid walls, which appeared to have been painted with swimming pool paint. Or perhaps all white? There was something about an all white room. But that would go better in the kitchen, she decided.

She glanced up at the cat, but it had not moved. How amazingly different the room felt, Tammy mused, with another living occupant. It seemed, somehow, to take the edge off the silence, as though the sharp sounds of loneliness were muffled by fur.

***

Next morning the cat had gone, presumably back the way it had come, through the broken pane. Tammy, who'd woken early and rushed to the sitting room in her pyjamas, felt oddly let down, but told herself briskly that it was a good thing, too, and

Vanessa must have been terribly worried. The cat had still been asleep when she'd called it a night at eleven-thirty, and she'd gone to bed, guiltily aware that it was now too late to call anyone, and even more guiltily hoping the cat might stay all night, and perhaps even come and join her in bed. But the chair was starkly empty, with only a patch of black fur to show that the whole thing hadn't been a dream.

Vanessa was at home when Tammy rang her pretentious, gold-plated doorbell. She greeted Tammy with cries of rapture and ushered her into a pastel blue kitchen with neutral-toned furnishings. The round, glass-topped table held a vase of flowers in various shades of pink, clearly a florist's bouquet. It would be very easy to hate Vanessa, Tammy thought, but couldn't quite manage it in the face of Vanessa's cheerful friendliness.

'I had a little visitor last night,' she said. 'A cat, I thought it must be yours?'

Vanessa shrieked with horror. 'A cat? Heavens no, I can't stand cats. Always scratching the furniture and sicking up everywhere. Can't have a bar of them. Why did you think it was mine?'

'Well, it had this really fancy collar on, all over diamonds, well I suppose they'd be crystals really, but it looked so decoratey, kind of thing...' Tammy trailed off, embarrassed.

'Well, it certainly isn't mine. I don't know whose it would be, either. Milk and sugar?'

'Just milk, thanks. You've no idea at all whose it might be, then? It was quite small, black with white paws and a white front.'

Vanessa shrugged. 'No idea. I've never seen one like that around here, though. Did it go away again?'

'Yes, it was gone when I woke up this morning.' Tammy stirred her coffee thoughtfully. 'I suppose it was just checking out the new arrival.' She was surprised at the pang of loneliness she felt at the thought that she might not see the cat again.

***

The cat appeared again that night, and also on the two following nights, staying till about ten-thirty each time. Tammy fell into the habit of watching out the front window every evening for it to appear. Although it never arrived earlier than a few minutes past eight, she would start looking hopefully out every few minutes as soon as it got dark. As soon as it arrived, she'd pour out a saucer of milk (the cat liked only chocolate milk, she'd discovered when it'd hopped up on the table and calmly helped itself out of her glass) and settle down for a nice long chat. She told the cat, whom she addressed variously as Princess, Sweetie and FluffyBum, all about Neville, the early days of their love, how perfect it had been, and all about how she'd caught the cheating fucker boffing her friend Maureen, right on her own kitchen table when she'd come home unexpectedly because her yoga class had been cancelled. She recounted the sad history of the death of their marriage, the fruitless attempts at counselling, where the counsellor had taken Neville's side and basically said the whole thing was her fault for not being more sexually adventurous, and digressed into a discussion of those more perverse of Neville's inclinations that she'd never been able to bring herself to gratify. She shared her dreams for the future, of finding True Love with a Real Man, who must be out there somewhere, after all, mustn't he Princess, there's someone for everyone. She confessed her guilty fantasies of revenge, and some that were not fantasies (she'd been reading About Three Authors at the time, and when she had moved out it had seemed a shame not to leave a few prawns in the pelmets). She told the cat how hard it was being suddenly celibate when she'd been married all those years, especially on hot nights, and this far north, all the nights were hot.

Basically, she spilled her guts.

And then on Sunday night, the cat didn't come.

She waited and waited, hovering at the front window until it was too dark to see and then turning on the outside light, but no little black face appeared, no soft padding steps were heard. She watched until almost midnight before she gave up and went sadly to bed, to sleep a thin, unsatisfying sleep, waking every hour to toss restlessly and shed a few hopeless, meagre tears. It didn't help that there seemed to be a lot of cars driving up to Vanessa's house. Every time a door slammed, it jolted her back into wakefulness.

By the time her phone alarm burst into cheerful song on Monday morning, Tammy was a wreck. She dragged herself to the bathroom and stared hopelessly at the dark circles under her eyes. God, she looked like she'd been on a three day drunk. She had to start work at Safeway in less than two hours. Bloody Vanessa with all her visitors. The last one had left at three a.m. What the hell was she doing entertaining men at that hour with her husband away? The three cars Tammy had seen had each contained one man, who went quietly round to the back of the house. Weird. Tammy could envisage her having a bit on the side while her husband was on a long trip, but three different men?

Vanessa seemed far too fastidious to be an out-and-out slag like Neville. She wondered if he'd ever discovered the prawns.

*** 

After a gruelling day stacking shelves under the eagle eye of Shona the supervisor, Tammy felt like running a hot bath and slitting her wrists. Shona was a psychopath, Tammy was sure of it. All day she had followed Tammy about, staring critically at everything she did, which made Tammy nervous and caused her to drop things. Who could have imagined that it was imperative to line up the cans so that all the pictures on the fronts were perfectly aligned? Every time Shona had wanted to 'correct' her, she'd moved in to stand so close she was almost touching her, and stroked her arm, smiling in that nauseatingly passive aggressive way that means 'I hate you and I am going to make your life a misery,' and wafting great drafts of sickly chemical chewing-gum breath into her face. Tammy was in despair at the thought of having to go back there tomorrow, let alone every day for the foreseeable future.

She looked around at her empty, bare house, breathing with relief the strong scent of tea tree oil that still lingered. At least it was clean. And hers, or would be as soon as settlement went through. It seemed a sad little triumph now. Why had she imagined it would be so easy to reboot her life? How had she planned to earn a living, if not by this kind of menial job? The dole office man had been right; a degree in Fine Arts didn't fit one for economic survival all by itself. If only she'd a teaching qualification, she might have got on at one of the schools. There were three high schools in Yarrangong. Teaching English to snotty teenagers hadn't been her life's dream either, but it would certainly have been a big improvement on Shona and the science of baked bean alignment.

What had her life's dream been, exactly? Tammy found she couldn't really remember. She'd met Neville straight out of uni, and then it had all been about him, really. At the time she'd thought it was love's dream, like a movie, and she'd tried so hard, learning to cook and liking all his Navy friends, even the most empty-headed of them. In the first year of their marriage, she'd missed the coffee bars and late, late talk-fests with her university friends with an intensity that had been almost physical. Sometimes the need to talk about something other than football and childcare had burned in her like a cancer. She had tried a few times to connect with people on the base, but they'd never read anything, and when she'd mentioned the Romance of the Rose to one new friend and been told her friend 'didn't have time for reading Mills and Boon' and that neither would Tammy once she had a baby, she had given up. Gradually, without noticing, she had stopped reading anything meatier than James Patterson. Her brain, once the envy of her Post-Modernists class, lay fallow.

She needed to take charge again, she realised as she lay back in the bath. She'd thought she'd done that, but she'd only been reacting. Have to leave the marital home, get a house. Have to earn money, get a job. Reacting. Not proacting, if that was indeed a word. She needed to proact. Take charge, properly, of her life. Having a goal, that was the thing. All through uni, she'd had the goal of her ultimate graduation with First Class Honours. She'd achieved that, so she wasn't a complete failure. Her trouble had been laziness, she realised with a pang. She'd allowed Neville to take over her world, accepting a secondary role in her own life.

She needed a life goal again, to make her a full person. But she was so tired, and the hot water was so good... the cat. That was something. She'd passively let her come and go, and she'd just gone, and left her, evidently finding her wanting just as Neville had done.

'Right,' Tammy said out loud, sitting up and reaching for the soap. If the cat ever did come again, she would keep her there, and take her to the vet. Get her microchip read. She'd be able to find out whose cat she was then, and if the owner couldn't be contacted, she'd have defacto possession and could look into getting it transferred to herself. It was a plan, not a very big one, but it felt good all the same.

As she cooked her solitary stirfry, though, it seemed like a rather empty victory. Once again there was no sign of the cat. Just in case, though, Tammy dragged one of the still-not-unpacked boxes of books from the spare bedroom and positioned it next to the front door. If the cat did reappear, she'd quickly slide it in front of the hole, trapping the cat inside. It could stay the night and she'd take it to a vet the next day, as soon as she got off from work.

The cat didn't come back that night, though, or the next, and Tammy had almost given up when the little black head slipped quietly through the broken pane and the cat poured itself into the room and padded quietly over to the sofa.

Quick as a flash, Tammy was over to the door, shoving the box in front of the pane with her foot, a wide, wide grin splitting her face. What a blessing that she'd prepared for this moment, she exulted as she hauled out from the pantry cupboard the plastic litter box and sack of kittyflakes she'd brought home from the supermarket, using her staff discount. Now, where to set it up? Not in the kitchen, she thought. Not right where she cooked and ate. The bathroom would be the best place. No, the lavatory. She didn't want to smell fresh cat poo while she was brushing her teeth in the morning. There was just enough room in the lavatory, and that was, after all, the correct place for calls of nature.

Now, food. Princess would require breakfast and would have to spend the day before Tammy got out of work and could take her to the vet, so she'd bought a sample packet of eight small boxes of different flavours of cat biscuits, and a selection of Fancy Feast tins. Surely something would take the cat's fancy, and if not, it would only be less than twenty-four hours before she was in touch with her family, and they could come and get her.

Princess, as usual, disdained every food she was offered, but settled happily enough on the sofa with Tammy. She must already have eaten, Tammy supposed. Anyway, she'd shown her the litter box, and later on she'd show her the bed.

At eleven-thirty, Princess suddenly left off washing her paws, sat up and stared alertly towards the door. Presently she ran to the door and pawed at the box, looking back at Tammy and letting out a plaintive mew. That was sudden, Tammy thought. It was almost as if she'd heard something.  Could her owner be calling her a few streets away, out of earshot to humans but clearly audible to a cat's superior senses? Well, never mind. It was only one night, and then they'd know where she was, and Tammy could relax. Uneasily, she suppressed the thought that once they knew she'd been with Tammy every night, they'd keep her in and stop her from visiting. That wasn't her problem. Her problem was to make sure Princess was being properly looked after, and then if she had to say goodbye, well, so be it.

Princess continued in an agitated state, on and off, until two in the morning, and then seemed to accept her confinement. Tammy took her off to bed, and woke in the morning to a face full of warmly heaving black fur.

She left for work by the back door, so as not to disturb her arrangement of the box at the front, and counted every minute until her shift finished, not even minding the sleazy stroking of her arms and the blasts of chemical strawberry from Shona's toxic breath, hardly noticing them in fact, because her mind was full of the fact that she had someone to go home to, even if it was for just this once.

***

The vet surgery was not busy, and Tammy was able to go straight in. Not having a cat carrier, she'd put Princess in the laundry hamper and tied the lid down with a bit of string. It was awkward lugging it in from the car, and the receptionist gave her an odd look, but Tammy was On A Mission. What were these minor inconveniences? She disregarded them.

The vet, a kindly-looking older man, greeted her warmly as she lifted Princess from the basket. 'Hello, Tom! What have you been up to, eh?'

'It's Tammy,' she corrected him.

The vet looked up from Princess. 'What, sorry?'

'It's Tammy. My name. Not Tom.'

The vet laughed. 'Oh, sorry, I was talking to Tom, here. We know him well, he's been a patient all his life. You must be new on the squad.'

'Squad? What squad? I just brought her in to get her microchip read so I can contact her people. She's been hanging out at my house every night for a week, and I worry that she's lost or something.'

The vet ran the microchip reader over the cat. 'Well, in the first place, it's he, not she. Tom by name and Tom by nature.' He chuckled. 'He really ought to have been desexed, but you know what young men are like.' A small printer in the corner whirred and spat out a sheet of paper, which he handed to Tammy. 'There you go. All present and correct, and I'm sure they'll be happy to know where he's been spending his time.'

'So, you know the people?' Numbly, she took the paper. All the time, she realised, she'd been hoping for a negative result. Hoping that Princess (Tom, she sadly corrected herself) could stay with her forever. That she'd have someone of her own, someone to love again. Someone who wouldn't cheat on her on her kitchen table with her so-called best friend. Who would, in fact, *be* her best friend. Someone of her own. Tears blurring her eyes, she looked at the paper.

'Hang on, this can't be right. It says she's – he's – registered to the police. How can that be? The police don't own cats. Dogs, yeah, but cats?'

'It's some kind of special operation taskforce. Don't ask me how it works, in fifty years of practice I don't remember hearing a single instance of a cat doing useful work, other than the odd bit of pest control, of course. Work just isn't what cats do.'

***

The sheet the vet had given her had a mobile number, and a contact name. Detective Senior

Constable Ben Jackson. Tammy fortified herself with a strong cup of tea before dialling.

'You have called Detective Senior Constable Ben Jackson. I'm unable to take your call at the moment. Please leave your name and number. If you require urgent police assistance, hang up now and dial triple zero. Thank you.' Beep.

'Um, hi, this is Tammy, Tammy Norman. Look, I'm calling because I've got this cat here, Tom, you were listed on his details, on his microchip. Can you give me a call back, please. Thanks. Bye.'

She had hung up, sweating with embarrassment, before she remembered she hadn't left her number, and had to ring up again.

***

The call came shortly before eleven next morning, but Tammy couldn't answer it, with Shona spying on her as usual from the end of the aisle. She had to wait until her twelve-thirty lunch break before she could play back the message.

Detective Senior Constable Ben Jackson had received her message and wanted to come and fetch his cat. He hoped she hadn't been inconvenienced. If she could phone him back with the address, he'd be right over.

Tammy called back and arranged for him to come at six. She'd be able to get home easily by five, but secretly, she wanted to have one last hour with Princess. Tom, she reminded herself. She'd probably never see him again once the cop took him away. She sniffed back her feelings and went back inside to stack the dairy case. At least he sounded nice, she tried to comfort herself. The voice on the phone had sounded young and pleasant, even friendly. She hoped she hadn't committed some criminal offence by retaining his cat.

***

By driving as fast as she dared, she made it home at twenty to five. Good; she'd have those extra minutes with Tom before the man came to take him away. She let herself in the back door, calling out for him until he came bounding out of the kitchen. She snatched him up and buried her nose in the soft fur, huffing his strong cat scent until she thought her lungs would burst.

Eighty minutes, she had with him. Eighty minutes. They'd make the most of it.

A game of string occupied the first half hour, and then they settled on the sofa for a cuddle. After the first few times, Tammy refused to look at her watch. She wasn't going to spoil their last hour together by overthinking. She took off the watch and stuffed it into her pocket, out of temptation's way. Time passed unremarked as she closed her eyes and lost herself in the sensation of soft fur pressed against her cheek, and the rumbling vibration of purrs, and the sharp, almost-but-not-quite painful pinpricks of kneading on her chest. Tears leaked unnoticed from the corners of her eyes, but Tammy didn't feel sad. She had locked onto the present moment, and was hanging on to it for her life.

She jumped when the doorbell rang, and Tom leapt off her, gouging small, stinging tracks on her stomach where he'd been lying. Scrubbing her hands over her face and through her uncombed hair, she tried to collect herself, but the jolt of adrenalin had settled in the pit of her stomach and made her knees feel wobbly as she forced herself up off the sofa and walked the few steps (the long mile) to the door. Time seemed to stretch out as she fumbled with the handle, and opened it to reveal...

Oh. My. God. The stranger standing on her doorstep was not at all what she'd expected. Tammy's idea of a police detective was a fattish, middle-aged man, badly dressed and not very handsome. But this one... oh, wow. Tall but not too tall, dressed in a suit and open-collared shirt. Sexy

Clark Kent glasses offset a fine-boned, almost too delicate face, and just a hint of manly stubble. And a long, flat stomach, going down to a low-slung belt without even a hint of paunch.

The stranger opened his perfect, chiselled lips. Intent on the flash of toothpaste-commercial teeth, Tammy missed what he actually said. She was sure she caught 'Jackson', though. That was the cop's name, wasn't it?

Tammy's mind was a blank. What was she... oh, yes. He'd come to take Tom away. She fumbled for the words. 'Come... come in...' She stepped back to allow him entrance. 'He's right here.'

'So I see, so I see, the little mongrel.' He addressed himself to Tom, sprawled upside down on the sofa. 'What's the idea, eh? Goofing off on the job. Putting this nice lady to all this trouble. Although,' he grinned up at Tammy, 'I can't really say I blame you.'

They'd be out of here in a moment. Tom, her little friend, would be out of her life forever, and this glorious man... Tammy found she wasn't ready to let the vision of loveliness go, either. Now that she'd got her heart rate down and her eyes focusing again, he was just the prettiest thing she'd seen in ages, except for Tom, of course, she hurriedly corrected herself. After all, no one is ever as beautiful as a cat. Stands to reason, after all... Shut up, stupid, she chastised herself. Stop babbling and get your act together.

'Would you like... a coffee? I was just about to...'

Jackson looked up from the tummy rubs he was giving Tom. 'Never say no to a coffee! That'd be great, thanks.' His smile was as wide as the ocean, his eyes guileless.

'So,' he went on as he settled himself at the kitchen table, 'I see you've moved into the old Booker house.'

'Booker... oh, the people. I didn't know them. This house... it was all I could afford. It was cheap...'

'I'll bet it was, the state it must have been in. Some of my mates were on the raid. So you didn't know them then, the Bookers?' He leaned back in his chair and seemed to relax.

'Not at all, I've just come up from Melbourne, I don't really know anyone here.' The coffee machine screeched its cry of bounty and she ejected the pod and reloaded for her own cup. 'I looked all over, and I really picked this town because of the cheap house, I have to admit. I mean, it was incredibly cheap, and I couldn't afford much after...'

'What? Hey, nice coffee. Divorce, was it?'

'Yes, how did you know?'

He shrugged. 'I'm a detective. We can tell these things. Actually, it's kind of obvious. You've got hardly any furniture, and you've still got a dent on your ring finger.'

Tammy sat down with her own coffee. 'Well anyway, yes, it was a divorce, not very nice and I've come up here to start over. I've got this house and a job, well a sort of a job, it's pretty awful but it'll put food on the table until I find something decent, and, well I almost thought I was going to have a cat until...' she trailed off miserably, remembering why he was there.

'So you and Tom hit it off pretty well, hey?'

'Oh yes, I love him, he's the most beautiful little cat. It's been wonderful having him here, you can't imagine what it's like, just having someone else there...' She felt herself getting teary, and cast about for a diversion. 'Um, sorry I don't have any biscuits, I don't keep any in the house, too much temptation on the long evenings if you've got a packet of Tim Tams in the cupboard, you know.' Stop it, she told herself. You're babbling again.

Talk about something sensible, for God's sake. 'So, how come the police force have got a cat? I never heard of that before.'

For the first time, Jackson seemed ill at ease. And was that a blush? Yes, it was! A tide of red swept up his neck and suffused his face, making the grey eyes look almost green. Tammy put her elbows on the table and leaned forward. She knew she was about to hear something really good. Was Tom a private cat, that he'd registered to the police for some weird reason?

'It's a special operation. Quite new. It's called, um,' his voice trailed off into a mumble.

'What? Sorry, I didn't catch that.'

Jackson cleared his throat, looking shifty. 'Operation Tomcat,' he said defiantly.

Tammy couldn't help herself. She roared with laughter. 'Operation Tomcat? What do you do, go round and spray on the crims?'

Jackson was crimson now. 'I know, I know, it's hilarious. This is my life now,' he added bitterly. 'No, it's ok, go ahead and laugh, everyone else does.' He grinned ruefully. 'Used to myself till I got posted to it.'

'Well come on, you can't leave it there, I want

to know all about it.'

Jackson took a deep breath and a swig of coffee, and seemed to square his shoulders.

'See, it's a new department. Experimental. Using alternative surveillance and investigation techniques.'

'What's it called?'

Jackson, whose colour had receded slightly, reached a new depth of scarlet intensity at this question. He stared down at the table. 'Tactical Watch Alternative Taskforce,' he said miserably.

This was too much for Tammy. She completely lost it. When she managed to get her breath back, she repeated, 'Tactical Watch Alternative Taskforce. Oh my God. So... you're The Man From TWAT.' She dissolved into hysteria, only getting a grip when she realised Jackson's hunched posture and silence indicated real misery. Snorting a little, she caught her breath and reached out a sympathetic hand to pat his wrist.

'I'm so sorry, Senior Constable Jackson. You must get this all the time. It must be awful, and I'm really sorry I added to it.'

He pulled himself together. 'Nah, it's okay. Don't worry about it. I'm used to it. And I've got to admit, it is funny. Just not so much when you're in it yourself. Anyway, it's Ben, call me Ben. And you're Tammy, right?'

Tammy nodded. 'So tell me about this new operation. I promise I won't laugh again.'

'Well, the thing is that some bright spark at Headquarters reckoned the crims are pretty good at avoiding all the usual means of surveillance, and the idea was to develop new methods of gaining police intelligence that aren't known or suspected. You know, wacko stuff.'

'What, like that TV show? Fringe?'

'Kind of. That's what Operation Tomcat is. See Tom there, you might have noticed he's got rather a fancy collar on.'

'Yes, I did notice. It seemed a bit unusual for a cat that roams around the streets.'

'Well, let me tell you, Tammy, that collar is a marvel of technology.'

'The collar? How?'

'Miniaturised electronics. That collar has a tiny camera and voice recorder in it, with a transmitter that sends on a tight beam back to the receiving station. We can track him using GPS and know exactly where he is, and everything he sees and hears, we see and hear.'

Tammy digested this in silence for a few moments.

'But why? I mean, what's the point of watching him hunt mice or whatever? Surely you don't sit there watching him just in case he sees a burglary or something?'

'Ah, well, that's the fiendish cunning of it, see.' Ben's eyes lit up with enthusiasm. 'We direct him to the place where we want him to go by rubbing aromatic substances.'

'Aromatic substances?' Tammy could feel the pressure of laughter building in her chest, but sternly reminded herself that she'd promised. 'So what, you go round the crims' lairs and spray Old Spice on the doorknob? Don't they tend to notice that?'

'No, we use a special catnip spray they developed in America. It's undetectable by humans. And delivery is achieved by means of unsuspected personnel.'

'What's that mean?'

'Well, there are always people who go places and don't get noticed. The postman, for instance.

Nobody notices the postman delivering letters. You see the guy in his yellow kit stop at your letterbox, you don't really look at him, do you? Well, see, sometimes that won't be the regular postman. If you're on our list, that is. And while he's shoving letters and junk mail in the box, he delivers a little squirt of this stuff. And that attracts Tom to the house.'

'Does this actually work?'

There was a silence.

'Work... well, it sort of worked in the field trials. Up to a point.'

'But in practice? In real life? I mean, have you caught any criminals this way?'

'Well, not exactly, not as such, no, not yet. But it's early days. And we've obtained some very interesting information. Very interesting indeed.'

'Like what?'

Ben looked smugly triumphant. 'I'm not at liberty to say.'

'So how did you get into this special division? Have you always been interested in alternative police techniques?'

The red tide was rising again. There seemed to be no limit to the amount of embarrassment she was inflicting on this poor man. Tammy felt a little sorry, but not sorry enough to dampen her curiosity.

'Not so much... I was a normal detective before. Well, it's a small town, you're bound to hear sooner or later, I suppose. See, the thing is, nobody wants to go in TWAT. I mean, would you? So it's more or less... not exactly disciplinary, as such, but when you've fucked up. People get sent there when they've screwed up big time, and I guess I did that right enough.'

Tammy patted his wrist again. He looked so unhappy that it didn't really seem funny any more.

Ben raised his head and looked her in the eyes. 'It was a servo robbery. That big service station on the Bentsville road. It would have been okay, the guy working there had one of those alarms under the counter, and the call came out on the radio – thing is, I was right there. I mean, I was filling up my car when the call came through. The radio was turned right up and the getaway guy heard it and started blasting his horn, the armed guy came belting out to jump in the car and there was just no time, no time to wait for backup or anything, they were getting away and I yelled Stop Police but they didn't, and... I drew my weapon.'

He sighed and scrubbed at his face with both hands.

Tammy felt tears of sympathy pricking the backs of her eyes. She clutched his hand.

'Did you... kill someone?'

Ben barked out a laugh. 'Not hardly. I tripped over the air hose and shot myself in the leg. The robbers got away. They got twenty grand, and we never managed to pick them up. Whoever they were, they just got away clean.'

'I don't get why that's your fault, though. I mean, you did what you could, there was only you, surely that could have happened to anyone?'

'You don't get it. I had the police radio turned right up, because I'd been listening to music in the car. We're not supposed to do that, it's not to be heard by non-members. So I was the one who tipped them off, by doing that. There were a couple of other units on the way, if they hadn't heard the radio we'd have probably caught them. So you see, you're looking at a royal screwup, and that was my ticket to TWAT.'

Tammy didn't know what to say. She was filled with a sense of the inevitability of events. If her yoga class hadn't been cancelled that day... if she'd done the shopping instead of going straight home... and Jen Miles had wanted her to go round and visit, but she hadn't felt like it... if she'd only been a better friend, she'd still be happily married. If poor Ben had not listened to his music on the job... her head spun thinking about it. Best not to think about it. You had to do what you could, where you were, with what you had, that had always been Tammy's philosophy.

'So who are you after now? The Mr Big of Crime?'

'Not exactly, but it is rather an important operation. See, someone's dealing meth in all three of the high schools. We don't know who it is or how they're delivering, but we think we know who the distributor is. So we're hoping to get something on the scumbag.'

'Someone around here, then? God, you didn't suspect me, did you?'

'No, although we do like to check out the new arrivals, but you had no record or anything. No, this character's a few houses down from you. He's actually listed as the owner of this house, that was why I asked if you knew the former tenants.'

'Oh my God, Fred Steiner. He's still my landlord, I'm waiting for my divorce settlement to come through so I've got a temporary rental agreement pending settlement on the property sale. And he's the worst, he won't do anything, fix anything – I know perfectly well he's supposed to be responsible for repairs until settlement goes through, but look at that pane of glass in the front door, that happened at the start of last week, and he still hasn't done anything about it. That's how Tom's been coming in.'

Ben flashed her a cheeky grin. 'No rain without some sunshine, then. I wouldn't have met you.'

Oh my God. Was he flirting with her? Could it be?

'So then, if you've got this aromatic spray and all that, how come he's been coming here instead?'

'Dunno.' Ben scratched his head. 'That's a bit of a mystery, that is. Only thing I can think of is, well this house is kind of fragrant, don't get me wrong, it's a nice clean smell, but I'm just wondering if that sort of overrode the other stuff.'

'It's tea tree oil. The place smelled terrible when I moved in. The matting in the front room stank of pee, and someone had been sick in one of the bedrooms and not cleaned it up – I basically spent the whole first week scrubbing everything with Domestos and tea tree.' She looked ruefully at her still-scruffy cuticles.

'Domestos, that's bleach, isn't it? That might explain it. Ammonia. As it breaks down, it gives out a smell that to a cat, resembles cat urine.'

'I suppose.'

'We might have to adjust our formula.'

'Yeah.'

A silence fell.

'Well,' said Ben, getting to his feet, 'It's been really great chatting, but I'd better get Tom back to where he's supposed to be. Duty calls and all that.'

At that moment, a thought struck Tammy with the force of a tornado.

'Hang on a minute. You said he was beaming transmissions all the time. But he's been here all the... Oh. My. God. He was in the bathroom with me. He likes to sit on the edge of the bath and dip his paws in the water– oh, shit. Have you been watching me in the bath? You pervert!'

Once again, the crimson tide rose. He wouldn't be much good at undercover work, Tammy thought. Gave himself away far too easily. But then, it didn't seem like he was all that great at police work generally, so the problem would hardly be likely to arise.

'No way known, no way, we didn't watch that. No, soon as we saw he was in the wrong house, we stopped watching, honest.'

'Who is WE?'

'Well, me and my mate. There's always two of us on an op, one to drive, you know, and one to work the equipment. You know us cops always work in pairs. There's got to be an informant and a corroborator, when we make an arrest, and stuff.'

'And another thing,' Tammy continued, hitting her stride. 'You said you had GPS on that thing. Why didn't you come and tell me as soon as you knew where he was? Why did I have to trap him inside and get his microchip scanned and ring you up to find all this out? I had to pay for that, you know. And another thing–'

Ben was backing away, hands raised in surrender. 'I fully realise how you've been inconvenienced. The Department will reimburse you for the vet's bill, if you just give me your receipt, I'll take care of it for you. I promise you, we didn't look at the footage, we turned it off every time.'

'Why didn't you know where he was?'

'The GPS isn't that accurate with just one station, we'd have had to have a second car to narrow it down to a particular house. We knew he was around here somewhere, we've been releasing him from just around the corner. And then we call him back with the dog whistle. He's been trained to respond to that.'

'God! How did you train a cat to come to a dog whistle? I bet it was cruel. You bastard.'

'Calm down, Tammy, it wasn't cruel, we train him using treats, little dried fish, that's all.'

'And what about the voice recordings? Oh God,' Tammy wailed as memories of the conversations she'd had with her little friend surged up in her memory.

Ben sniggered.

'Oh my God! Are you laughing? Those were private conversations, you had no right...'

'Look, calm down, please, we didn't listen to any of it. We knew he was in the wrong place, so we just scrubbed the recordings.'

Tammy narrowed her eyes. 'You wouldn't have known he was in the wrong place the whole time unless you looked at it all.'

'Only on fast forward, honest.' He sniggered again. 'Your secret is safe with us.'

'Secret? What secret?'

'About the prawns in the curtain pelmets. You don't have to worry about that. You didn't commit any offence as you were still residing in the premises at the time. Sounds like the cheating fucker got what he deserved anyway. You're a bit of a hero down the watchhouse actually.'

Tammy sank onto the sofa and buried her face in her hands. Tom, waking from his nap, hopped onto her lap and nosed at her fingers, emitting small chirps of affection.

Ben sat next to her and patted her back. 'Look, I really am sorry, you've had your privacy invaded and it wasn't our fault, but I'd like to make it up to you. How about dinner on Saturday night? There's a really flash Italian restaurant just opened in town, it's supposed to be fantastic. Whatta ya say?'

Tammy blinked. 'You're asking me out? Just to say sorry?'

'Well, yeah. I feel like I ought to make it up to you, and also to thank you for taking good care of our little operative here. Come on, it'll be nice.'

'Well, alright. As long it's not a date date.'

Ben looked shocked. 'Of course not. Just community relations, cross my heart. Well, come on, Tiger.' He scooped up Tom and dropped him into the carrier. 'Duty calls.'

He turned at the door. 'I'll pick you up at seven-thirty Saturday. Wear something special.' He waggled his eyebrows and was gone, leaving Tammy feeling shell-shocked.

***

Tammy had been to the hairdresser, and her normally unruly hair hung in shining, ordered waves past her shoulders. She'd finished unpacking and dug out her sexiest dress, the one, she bitterly remembered, that had always got Neville into such a state. A fresh set of porcelain nails adorned her newly conditioned fingers. The credit card would never be the same again – in fact it was a wonder it hadn't spontaneously combusted – but she'd wanted everything to be right for this, her first evening out in more than eighteen months. Of course it wasn't a real date, she reminded herself, but she could pretend, couldn't she? And Tammy was pretending for all she was worth. This was Her Night.

The waiter fluttered about, draping starched napkins, mindlessly reciting the special dishes and chattering away. Tammy tuned him out and looked at Ben. In the candlelight, he looked even more enticing. She felt parts of herself that had lain dormant for many months stir into life.

'So, did you–'

'I was wondering–'

'Oh, sorry, go on.'

'No, that's ok, you go.'

It was the usual First Date Awkwardness. FDA, Tammy and her friends had called it at uni. If he kissed her goodnight, probably their noses would clash, too. If he kissed her... Tammy dragged her mind back to the present. She had to stop thinking like this, keep in mind that however much she wished it to be otherwise, this was definitely not a date, it was, what had he said? Yes, community relations, he was just taking her out to make up for having video-recorded her in the bath and eavesdropped on her private gutspill conversations. No, don't start thinking about that again. Get your mind off that, you'll get nervous and probably spill wine everywhere or something. Say something intelligent, for God's sake. Something classy.

'I don't think it's him.' Shit. What was that about? She'd meant to say something clever, not just blurt out the first thing that came into her mind.

'What? Him who? What's not him?'

'The drug dealer. I don't think it's Fred Steiner.'

'Why not?'

'He never goes anywhere. He just sits on his front verandah all day drinking beer. I went over there yesterday to remind him about fixing the door, and he was already three sheets to the wind at five o'clock. He just wouldn't be together enough to do drug dealing, he wouldn't be able to count his change or measure powder or anything. And another thing. He never has any visitors or goes anywhere. So how would he be getting it?'

Ben thought about this for a moment. 'So, do you have any other suspect in mind?'

'Don't take the piss, I'm serious. Steiner is just too much of a drunken loser to co-ordinate an operation like that. Look, it's getting from the dealer into all three of the schools, so someone has to be taking it there, and they'd have to be getting it from him, and they just aren't. I mean, I live three doors from him and there's literally no traffic on our street most of the time.'

'I wasn't taking the piss, honest. Look, I'll

admit we haven't got much to go on. It was just the one kid, actually, we got him to the hospital after an overdose and he muttered something in the ambulance.'

'What? But he'd have been well and truly drug-fucked, he might have been hallucinating or anything.'

'Yeah, well that's the problem, see, and when he came round he wouldn't say anything, wouldn't talk to us at all.'

'Well, I don't see that you've got anything to go on at all, then. Are you even sure that's what the kid was actually talking about?'

Ben sighed. 'Not really.'

They left the subject then, in favour of the menu and wine choices, but it niggled at the back of Tammy's mind all through dinner. She felt there was some connection that she'd missed, something important that would support her firm idea that Fred Steiner, idle, drunken, non-door-fixing waste of space, was not the town drug pusher.

'Have you managed to get Tom to go into his house yet?' she asked over dessert (tiramisu for them both, with a bottle of champagne. She wondered in passing how a detective constable could afford this kind of meal, and also how a man with such beautifully flat abs could scoff down tiramisu with such gay abandon. He must have one of those metabolisms, she thought enviously, trying not to speculate about how the excess calories could be burned off).

'Nah, the little mongrel. He just makes a beeline for your house every night.'

'I haven't seen him.'

'I'm parking a bit closer now, where I've got a clear view down the street. I watch him through the night glasses and call him back. Sorry, Tammy, I know you'd like to see him, but he's supposed to be working. Look, tell you what, we're not on duty tomorrow, suppose I bring him over for a visit in the afternoon?'

'Oh, would you really? That would be lovely. I do miss him. I got so used to him, even in that short time.'

'Sure. Not a worry in the world. Tell you what, I'll grab a couple of videos too and we can order a pizza, how does that sound?'

Tammy's head spun even more than could be accounted for by half a bottle of Merlot followed by champagne. This had the sound of a real date, whatever tonight was. Play it cool, play it cool. He's probably just being friendly, because of Tom. Don't make a fool of yourself. Your own husband didn't want you, you stupid fat cow. This hunk certainly doesn't, he probably thinks of you as a sister. Just don't blow it, keep your pride intact.

'Yeah, okay,' she managed to croak out. 'Sounds good. D'you like Schwarzenegger?'

'What, you love Arnie too? This is starting to sound like a match made in heaven.'

Shut up, shut up, shut up, Tammy told herself. It was just a silly joke.

*** 

She was up early next morning, despite the champagne, filled with a searing energy that had her cleaning the house and hanging out all the washing before seven-thirty. She sorted out her tightest skinny jeans and a shirt that would conceal any muffin top that might make its appearance. Dress defensively, that was Tammy's motto. The thigh-length tunic had a nice casual look, too. The last thing she wanted to do was look like she was trying. A light spray of cologne and a hint of natural makeup, and she was ready. Only five hours too early.

She settled herself on the sofa with a book, a really good book, but couldn't concentrate. Every time a car drove past, she found herself looking out the window to see if it was Ben. *Don't be so stupid,* she told herself. *He won't even be waking up for hours.*

But it was only eleven-thirty when he arrived, freshly showered, with hair still wet and a sharp, lemony scent of cologne, bringing a bag of DVDs and a huge bunch of yellow roses, and Tom in his basket.

It was a magical day. This was how life ought to have been with Neville, Tammy thought hazily, a cool film on the box, sun streaming in, pizza with extra anchovies (how amazing was it that they both loved anchovies), a cat purring in her lap. Had it ever been like that, even in the beginning? She couldn't remember ever feeling so relaxed around Neville, even when they had been married for years. Somehow a little tension had always seemed to arrive like a breeze on his heels as he came in the door. When he had been off at work, those had been her relaxing times. In fact, she mused, propping her feet on Ben's lap and lying back on the sofa, she had actually, if she was honest, felt happier when he wasn't around.

When he leaned over and kissed her, she didn't

even open her eyes.

***

Tammy drifted through the next morning in a haze of happiness, arranging canned goods with gay abandon, pictures facing any which way. Some were even upside down. When Shona came bustling down Aisle Three in her pink smock, Tammy beamed at her.

Great happiness, however, does have this one terrible quality. It makes a person relax. Tammy was feeling relaxed, so very relaxed, in fact, that her inner censor completely failed to operate, and when Shona started her usual stroking of Tammy's arm, she jerked away, screaming 'Stop fucking groping me, you sick bitch!' at the top of her voice. Heads turned up and down Aisle Three, a hush settled over the store and someone dropped a jar of herrings with a small, explosive crash.

The resulting confrontation in the manager's office resembled an amateur rendition of Bohemian Rhapsody, threads interweaving in a demented polyphony:

**SHONA:** I'm just a poor supervisor, I was trying to help her, she doesn't know how to do anything, she's rude, she doesn't let me help her, poor me, I'm the victim here.

**TAMMY:** (*duplum*): She keeps *touching* me, it's creepy, she needs to learn to keep her hands to herself, nobody wants to be always getting pawed, it's disgusting.

**THE MANAGER:** (*triplum*): This has gone far enough, I can't have screaming and yelling in front of the customers, youse can both take this as your final warning.

The upshot was that Tammy was transferred to the night shift of shelf stackers, with immediate effect.

***

Night shift wasn't as bad as Tammy had expected. The store closed at ten, and after that it was quiet; the only sounds were the faint hum of the fluorescent lights and the occasional cheerful cries of the other night stackers, who all seemed to know each other and get on well. They were a scruffy-looking bunch, not particularly presentable and some with questionable hygiene, but Tammy found them restful, particularly the ones who didn't speak English. There was a supervisor, but he spent most of his time in the back office reading the paper, emerging only for the hourly 'smoke breaks' when everyone gathered around the delivery door, puffing away. Tammy didn't smoke, but felt the peer group pressure enough to carry her out there with them, although she felt a little shame-faced about it. She tried to stand upwind so the smoke wouldn't stink up her hair, without being obvious about it. Tomorrow she'd bring in a headscarf or something.

Tammy had a lot of time to think on night shift, the work being more or less purely mechanical (it didn't really take a lot of mentation to put cans the right way up, whatever Shona had thought), and found herself returning again and again to Ben's drug case. She was adamant in her belief that Fred Steiner was not the dealer, much as she disliked him and resented his failure to fix her door, and the feeling that she had some piece of information that would further support this idea didn't go away. Again and again she ran through the facts. It was known that children from all three high schools were obtaining meth. That was one indubitable fact, if only because there had been overdoses and hospital trips by children from all of the schools. This was why the case was considered of such urgency; it was only a matter of time before someone died. There had been an interview with one of the emergency doctors on the news last night.

Funny, Tammy mused, there hadn't been any mention of adult victims. Was it just that kids were more 'sexy' in the news sense, eliciting an extra level of sympathy? Children with drug overdoses were always portrayed as innocent victims, whereas an adult with the same problem tended to be viewed far less sympathetically. She must see what she could find out tomorrow. Or really, just ask Ben, she supposed, when she saw him next. He'd be bound to know. That reminded her; she must call him to cancel tomorrow's dinner; she'd invited him before yesterday's incident, and now, of course, she'd be having to start work at eight, which made dinner plans rather difficult. Perhaps they could make it a late lunch instead.

Glancing about to make sure the coast was clear, Tammy pulled out her mobile phone and stepped behind a display of chocolate. She had Ben on speed dial; alright, perhaps she was being a bit premature, but it wasn't like he'd know.

***

Ben was happy to make it lunch instead, and accordingly, the next day Tammy was once again curled on the sofa watching out the window. There went Vanessa again, loading huge plastic chests into her car for her Home Economics classes. Tammy wondered what sort of a teacher she was, and whether the kids liked her. What a lot of energy the woman had; she'd already been out once this morning, and now she had got back and taken in all the boxes and was busy loading up another batch.

What a lot of stuff she had to cart round. Surely the schools had their own cooking equipment? Was it all food? Why didn't they get it delivered at the school?

If she, Tammy, were going to teach cooking, she thought, she'd make sure all the pots and things were at the schools. What did they have budgets for, for heaven's sake? And all the ingredients would be delivered there too, and then she'd get the sixth form boys to lug it all up to her classroom or whatever. She certainly wouldn't be dragging enormous crates back and forth all day. Just packing them and unpacking them must be a nuisance. She'd have thought Vanessa would have been better organised.

Here was Ben now. She'd better get the lasagne in the oven.

***

'Gorgeous lasagne, Tammy. I must say, you're one hell of a cook.'

'Have some more?'

'I can't, thanks, now don't get me wrong, I would if I could, but three serves is my limit.'

'Coffee, then.'

'Ta.' Ben leaned back dangerously far in his chair and dangled his fingers for Tom, who was finishing off his own plate of lasagne, with extra cheese, under the table.

'Here you go.'

'Lovely, thanks. And did I mention, Ms Norman, you make a *great* cup of coffee.'

'We aim to please.' Tammy sat back down with her own cup. 'Actually, this is practically the only fancy thing I know how to make. You might get tired of it.'

'Never. Never, never, never. I solemnly swear –'

'–that I am up to no good–'

'No, no, I solemnly, solemnly and *sincerely,* no, stop laughing, have some respect, woman! I solemnly and sincerely swear, and declare and affirm, that I will never get sick of your lasagne, so help me God.'

'And Mrs Marsh.'

'Yes, so help me God and Mrs Marsh.'

'Seriously, though, I am rather limited in the cooking department. I ought to get some recipes from Vanessa.'

'Who's that, your sister?'

'No, Vanessa Carlson, she lives just over the road. What's the matter?' Ben had frozen, all hilarity gone. He was looking at her funny, a slitty-eyed, unfriendly look. A *cop* look, Tammy realised. As if he'd just caught her speeding through a red light. His voice, when he spoke, was cold.

'Know her well, do you?'

'Not really, but she's my neighbour, you know. Why, Ben?'

'I don't want you getting mixed up with them. They're bad news, her and her husband. Don't you know who he is?'

'He's some kind of business man, she said he was away on business.'

Ben snorted. 'Monkey business. He's in Port Phillip, doing three years for 15A.'

'What? Fifteen A what? And what's wrong with Port Phillip?'

'Tammy. Port Phillip prison. The maximum security prison?'

'What, he's in jail? Vanessa's husband? I don't

believe it, he can't be. She's so... '

'Tammy, I don't want you having anything to do with her. She's bad news. Trust me on this, they are not a bunch of people you want to get mixed up with.'

'Look, I think you're being a bit prejudiced, Ben. I mean, just because her husband's done some kind of white collar thingy, it doesn't mean *she's* evil, does it? Poor woman. Imagine the shame of it.'

'White collar – what are you talking about? I said section 15A. Intentionally cause serious injury in circumstances of gross violence.'

Tammy was diverted. 'Well, it would be, wouldn't it?'

'Come again?'

'Gross violence. I mean, if you seriously injured someone, you could hardly do it without being violent, could you?'

Ben clutched his forehead and muttered something not very nice under his breath.

'It's got a legal meaning. Look, Mario Carlson and his two mates held down a man and smashed both his kneecaps with a tire iron. Because he held out on some drug money. Now do you get it? Stay away from her. I mean it, Tammy.'

The words 'you're not the boss of me' rose to Tammy's lips, but she forced them back down again.

'See, this is why we're a bit lost on the drug situation,' Ben went on. 'Mario Carlson used to run all the drugs round here, but he's safely out of action, and so far as we've been able to find out, none of his known associates have moved into the area. So it's a new operation, whether it's a rival gang, or someone just saw an opportunity, or what, and the Drug Squad haven't come up with anything because they mainly work off people's records. And it looks like whoever's running this show hasn't got a record. Anyway, that's all well and good, but the Carlsons are bad news, and I would really appreciate it if you didn't have any more to do with them.'

Tammy went to the supermarket that night in a very sobered frame of mind. Ben was so handsome, and funny, and cute, and so, well, *nice* – she hadn't really thought about him being a cop after the first time they'd met. This new, grim view of him had her remembering how he'd got assigned to Operation Tomcat in the first place – because he had a *gun*, and was responding to an *armed robbery*. It was all a bit outside her comfort zone.

Had he had a gun on him that afternoon? No, surely not; she'd have felt it when she snuggled up to him, wouldn't she? Or would she? Tammy had never been out with anyone armed. Neville had worn a sword at his friend's wedding, but that had been purely ceremonial, and anyway, swords didn't count, they were like things from the movies. You never read about anyone being murdered with a sword. Or kids accidentally beheading themselves because someone left one lying about, or anything. Swords, Tammy felt, were essentially harmless. They belonged in the world of Ivanhoe, of Richard the Lionheart, not the real world. Guns, now... guns were different. Guns were murder, and terrorism, and sudden, violent death. Also, they made a loud bang, and if there was one thing Tammy couldn't bear, it was a sudden loud noise. Even a car backfiring several streets away could have her shrieking and jumping out of her skin.

***

Over the next few weeks, Tammy was too busy to worry much about Ben's concerns. She brought home her first paycheck from the supermarket, and found to her delight that after allowance had been made for rent and food, there was enough for paint. She chose a pale mushroom for the sitting room, with cream trim, and in every spare moment she sanded, scrubbed and filled cracks. Her appalling night job at the supermarket now appeared to her in a different, more kindly light, as there was absolutely no need to appear presentable for it, and her plaster-speckled hair and paint-spattered clothes fitted in well with the general air of not very clean neediness that characterised her workmates.

The days passed in a pleasant round of waking late and working on the walls, followed by a not-too-strenuous shift at the supermarket, a hot bath and bed. She had adjusted well to night work, and enjoyed falling asleep to the pre-dawn warblings of magpies and the cries of bats streaking homeward to their colony by the river. As she worked, her headphones delivered audiobooks of the works of Hope, Trollope and Scott, all downloaded free from Librivox. On her evenings off, Ben always seemed to be available, and they variously attended the local speedway, Latin dance night at the RSL Club, a party given by two of Ben's police friends, where Tammy was rigorously examined by at least fifteen people, and several restaurants.

The battered walls required a good deal of repair, and two coats of undercoat were needed to cover the ghastly aqua the former tenants had left, so it was not until the third week that Tammy prised open her can of colour.

She had left off her headphones for once,

wanting to experience to the full this, her first real act of transformation. The house, once a mere stopgap, a refuge of economic necessity, had now taken on for her a significance beyond its functions of shelter and comfort, and represented to her her precious independence, her safety, her complete freedom from reliance on another. It would become a place of great beauty, she vowed, a haven for body and spirit. And if ever she chose to welcome a second inhabitant, well... there were, after all, three bedrooms. Room, perhaps, for a couple, and a cat, and one day a child. Room to live, and love, and grow...

Tammy realised with a start that she'd been stirring for more than fifteen minutes, and reached for the roller tray.

As she painted, her thoughts drifted back to Ben, who was never, if truth were told, very far from her mind these days. Was she one of those women who always had to be with some man? She hoped not. She'd seen many of her university friends stuck in appalling relationships, held there by what had always seemed to her a completely unnecessary fear of being alone. And yet, what was the first thing she'd done when she'd been single? Jumped into another relationship herself.

There, that was the edges all done. Time for the

roller. Checking one final time for drips and loose brush hairs, Tammy descended the stepladder.

Of course, it hadn't been really immediate, she comforted herself. It had been a good eighteen months since she'd come home that fateful day and walked into her kitchen to find Maureen spreadeagled on the table, moaning as Neville, the cheating bastard, pumped away with his trousers round his ankles. Damn, there went a drip, running down. Catch it quickly before it starts to set. Too much paint on the roller.

It wasn't as if he wasn't keen, Tammy comforted herself. It wasn't like she was chasing after him or anything. He called to chat pretty well every afternoon, and by the way he was always available and wanting to go out on her nights off, she suspected he might have rearranged his schedule. And it wasn't like she'd gone looking for a man, like some people, signing up to those awful websites and claiming to be cuddly and have a GSOH, which meant you were hugely fat and a slapper with no manners. Now that really was desperate. Never in a million years would she go near one of those.

Thinking about it, Tammy decided, she was almost sure he'd rearranged his work schedule. Ben's work with Tom, silly as it was, did all happen at night, and it just didn't seem likely that a relatively junior cop would always have weekends off.

There, the first wall was done. Tammy set down the roller and stepped back to admire her achievement. It was a bit streaky in the top corner, but the second coat would take care of that, and she could always put on a third coat if necessary. How lovely it was going to look. She planned to accent it with dark blue curtains and rugs. The floor natural wood, of course, stripped and polished. If it was a bit old and hacked about, so much the better; it would add character.

How was that getting on, Tammy wondered as she started on the front wall. This one didn't have much area because of the big French windows, but then that also meant there were lots of edges to be carefully done first with the brush. The last she had heard, Tom had still been declining to go anywhere near Fred Steiner's house. They'd resorted to sneaking up at four in the morning and rubbing anchovies on the windowsills, but even this creative move had not been productive of any result. Tom, apparently, had, upon his release, invariably headed straight for Tammy's house, and cried outside the finally-fixed door. You'd think they'd know better, Tammy sniggered. Honestly, as if a cat was interested in what you wanted.

There went Vanessa again, loading up her car with another load of those big plastic boxes. How could she even lift them? And what on earth was in them?

And then.

The penny.

Dropped.

Tammy sat down suddenly, cross-legged on the floor, the loaded paintbrush delivering an unnoticed dollop of mushroom-coloured paint into her crotch. The boxes, those incessant, unnecessary plastic crates, being taken, day after day, week after week, to *all three high schools*. Going full, but not really that heavy, and coming back less full. No one would think anything of the home economics teacher turning up with her usual load of gear. No one would probably even consciously see her as she carried her deadly payload right into the classroom. And once there, how easy, how completely unremarkable, how *invisible* to ask particular children to see her after class. She wouldn't even need to ask them, Tammy realised, after the initial arrangements had been made. She probably had a few kids acting as distributors within each school.

It all made sense. The more she thought about it, the more sense it made. The Evil Drug Lord

(Tammy allowed herself the small luxury of thinking in terms of melodrama) trapped, disabled and languishing in Durance Vile. His Faithful Moll (alright, Vanessa wasn't exactly the moll type, but you had to have some artistic licence) loyally carrying on the family business in his absence. She'd have had the contacts to set everything up; in fact, whatever supplier she was dealing with might not even realise she was acting on her own and not on her husband's behalf. And in fact, she might not be. Suppose they'd been in it together right from the start, Vanessa not an innocent dupe but in fact a willing partner, perhaps even the instigator of the vile trade?

She had to get hold of Ben right away. Where was her phone? Wiping paint indiscriminately on jeans, shirt and the actual painting rag, she cast about for her handbag. Oh yes, she'd left it in the kitchen. Hold on, though, she ought to finish the bit she was doing and clean her tools. Yes, that would be best. But Vanessa might be poisoning some little kid even now. On the other hand, it would dry streaky. But it was only the first coat, so would that matter? But the paint would set in her brush and roller. She'd bought the best tools she could afford, and didn't want to have to replace them after only one use. But then the children.

Minutes ticked by and paint dried in the drip

tray as Tammy vacillated. Eventually, she pulled herself together and dumped roller, brush and tray into the laundry tub. They could soak in there.  She was drying her hands when the doorbell rang. Swearing under her breath, she rushed to the door, snatching up her bag on the way, and dumped its contents one-handed onto the sofa as she opened the door with her other hand.

There would be no need to hunt for her mobile phone, though. Ben stood on the step. He seemed to be struggling to hold back tears.

Everything flew out of Tammy's head as she wrapped her arms around Ben and steered him into the kitchen, murmuring soothing nothings. She got him into a chair and switched on the kettle for tea. Tammy was a great believer in tea as an instant remedy for all forms of emotional distress. It never did any harm, she felt, and often did good, even if it was just to make you stop panicking.

Ben had buried his face in his arms and was mumbling incoherently. She couldn't make head or tail of it. Never mind. Get the tea first. She slid a mug onto the table in front of him, teabag still dangling from it, and sat next to him, a hand on his shaking shoulders.

'Ben, whatever is it? What's happened?'

This elicited a stream of garbled talk, of which Tammy could only distinctly make out the word 'Tom', although the general tone of it seemed to be one of self-accusation.

'What's happened to Tom?'

Ben sat up, scrubbing at his face, pulling himself together with visible effort.

'Sorry to go off like this, Tammy. I just don't know what I'll do without the little bugger.'

'Do without – what d'you mean, he's not dead, is he?'

'No, but he might – he might die, Tammy, he's at the vet's now, they said they'd call me... I should never have brought him home. He's supposed to stay in his enclosure at the station when he's not working. He'd have been alright there.' He shook his head and reached for the mug, wrapping his hands around it as if to warm fingers numb with cold.

'Ben. What happened? Just try to tell me calmly.'

Ben sucked in a deep, if shaky, breath. 'Well, see, I've been taking him home after our shift. Like I said, he's supposed to stay in his quarters at the station, but I thought it was nicer for him in the flat, and then he's company, you know, and it seemed okay, I mean I got a litter box for him and everything, and he seemed happy with it.'

'Yes, right, so you took him home, and something happened? What happened, Ben?'

'It was when we got home this morning. We'd been on the usual stakeout, you know how it goes, he's supposed to –'

'Yes, yes, I know all that. What *happened*?'

'He just went completely weird. I mean, it was like he was trying to attack something that wasn't there, and when I spoke to him he didn't seem to know me, and he was dribbling, great strings of drool coming out of his mouth, and panting, and when I picked him up his heart was going like a thousand miles an hour, and he bit me, Tammy, he bit me.'

Tammy didn't know what to say. 'Do you have any idea what caused it?'

Ben shook his head hopelessly. 'None at all. I mean, I'd called him back, and he came, and I put him in his basket and drove home. I gave him some brekkie and he had that, and he settled down to wash himself, like he does, and then when I came out of the shower he was just in this state.'

'Could it have been the food, something wrong with the food?'

'I don't see how, it's just the same Whiskettes as every day. I only give him the dry in the morning because I'm going to sleep, see, and if I give him anything wet and he doesn't eat it all it gets flyblown.'

Ben's phone rang, shockingly loud in the small kitchen. Ben jumped and almost knocked over his tea. The phone rang again.

'Oh, shit, that'll be the vet.'

'Well go on, answer it.'

For a second Ben's tortured gaze met her own. 'What if he's...'

The phone rang a third time, and he snapped out of his panic and reached into his pocket. 'Ben Jackson.'

'Yeah.'

'Yeah.'

'No, he was fine, he was washing himself...'

'I see. Yes, right.'

'Right.'

'Right.' A deep sigh, with visible relaxing of posture.

'So he's going to be okay, you're sure...'

'Right. Yeah, of course. Thanks so much, Doctor.'

He disconnected and sat staring into space. Tammy tried to wait patiently, but after a few seconds could not refrain from shaking him.

'So what is it? Is he going to be alright?'

Ben sighed. 'Looks like it. They said he's stabilised and stopped carrying on, and they want to keep an eye on him till five o'clock and then if he doesn't get worse again he can go home.'

'Did they say what caused it?'

'Not really, but Doctor Wright thinks he might have stepped in something, some chemical, and then got a dose when he washed his feet. A stimulant reaction, he called it. They gave him something to make him sick, to empty everything out of his stomach, but Wright reckoned it might have been just traces of something.'

'What, like weed killer or something like that?'

'Yeah, I guess.' He laughed. 'Funny, really.'

'What's funny?'

'Well, the way he was, when I think about it, that's how people get when they O.D. with meth. The aggression, seeing things, all that.'

'You don't think–'

'What, that he found the factory and got himself a dose of product?' Ben considered this for a moment. 'Nah. Stuff like that doesn't happen in real life.'

But Tammy wasn't so sure. A memory flitted at the edges of her mind. A memory of seeing Tom, his fur glinting in the last of the daylight, picking his way along the top of Vanessa's fence, and streaking into her open garage as Tammy revved her engine to get over the broken kerb.

'Listen, Ben, there's something I wanted to talk to you about...'

***

Two hours and many cups of tea later, Tammy sat back, satisfied. She'd finally got it into Ben's thick head. Really, she thought, she was the one who should have been a cop.

Ben, however, although convinced by Tammy's arguments, was not enthusiastic about the prospect of bringing Vanessa to book.

'I just don't think I've got enough to get a warrant,' he repeated, his expression mulish.

'Why not? You've got a reasonable suspicion.'

Ben sighed. 'It's not the court that's the problem, Tam. It's the sergeant. See, only a sergeant or higher can apply for a search warrant. Normally, you go to the sarge, and he does the application to the court, he gets the warrant and off you go. Or someone else, whatever. I can't apply for a warrant because I'm not a sergeant. And I reckon I've got about two chances of convincing old Briginshaw to go for a warrant against Mrs Carlson. That would be Buckley's and None.'

'Why?'

'It's not her particularly. It's me. Remember why I'm in this squad in the first place? My name is mud. I'd never get him to listen. There's no actual evidence, after all, there's just this theory of yours. And remember, if it all goes pear-shaped, he's the one in the firing line. I mean, suppose we raid her and there's nothing, we're wrong. How does that look, especially after the Daily Constellation gets hold of it? Local Woman Raided, Claims Harassment. You know what they're like. I just don't need any more grief.'

'But what if you get this major drug ring, bust it up all by yourself and get a conviction? Then you'd be a hero. Local Cop Saves Our Kids.'

Ben grinned. 'You've been watching too much telly. There's no "all by yourself" in the real police. There's no heroics. It's just a job, a dirty job.'

Tammy sighed. Men. They just gave up so easily. She was sure there'd be a way. After Ben had left for the vet's, she got out her laptop.

***

It was right enough, she found, that only a sergeant or above could apply for a warrant; that was in the Drugs, Poisons and Controlled Substances Act. Undaunted, she turned her mind around to circumvent the restriction. What about searching without a warrant? She seemed to recall that evidence obtained illegally wasn't admissible in court, but then most of her knowledge of criminal law came from American television. Perhaps the law was different here? It certainly was in other ways.

Luckily for Tammy, the recently enacted Evidence Act was in plain English. She found, to her triumph, that the court had a discretion either to include or to exclude evidence obtained by improper means. Now, what could those means be?

She didn't see Ben cold-bloodedly breaking in and raiding Vanessa's house without any authority at all. In fact, she knew him well enough to be quite sure he wouldn't have a bar of it. To Tammy, the end justified the means when you were dealing with really bad people, but Ben had a stolid, by-the-book kind of mind, and he'd dig in his heels, she knew. And she'd get that patronising lecture about a policeman's Duty to Society, and all that.

So, how could she get him in there on a search without a warrant? What about a fake warrant? No, he'd never have anything to do with that, and he'd be in a world of trouble when the forgery was discovered. Idly, she went back to the Drugs Act. Schedule Ten had the form of the warrant, she discovered. It was all in terrible archaic language, but the only identifying information that seemed to be in it was the nature of the stuff being searched for and the address to be searched. Nothing about the occupant's name or anything.

Tammy leaned back and massaged her neck, stiff from hunching over the laptop. An idea was forming, best not to force it. Fred Steiner was at number sixteen. Vanessa was at number twelve. She stared at the ceiling. Number sixteen, number twelve... what if there were a mistake on the warrant? Easy to write the wrong number by accident. No one could ever really say for sure that it hadn't been an accident. Then the raid happens, yes, and finds the evidence, the still or whatever was used to make the stuff, or traffickable quantities and so on, and then, then it goes to court... and yes, the court has a discretion to include the evidence, and Tammy hardly thought they'd be likely not to, not when it was a major drug operation placing the lives of so many children at risk... Ben would be a hero, he'd get his old job back, Vanessa would go off to join her husband in the slammer, everybody would be happy. All he'd have to do would be to convince the sergeant to get a warrant for Fred Steiner's place, and surely that wouldn't be difficult as that was the house he'd been doing the surveillance on all that time, and come to think of it, trying to get Tom in there, which, Tammy thought, might well fall under the heading of an illegal search.

It was time to go to work. Tammy closed her laptop thoughtfully. She'd sleep on it, and talk to Ben tomorrow afternoon.

***

'Look, Tammy, you've just been watching too much telly. Too many of those Yank cop shows. It's not like that in real life. You can't just play around and get phony warrants issued to the wrong address and go in with guns blazing. There'd be hell to pay.

I'd probably get kicked out of the force. And rightly so, I might add. The public trusts us to act with integrity. There has to be confidence...'

It was the same lecture she'd heard several times before. High level of integrity blah blah blah ethical standards blah blah blah public confidence. Tammy tuned out.

***

Over the next few days, Tammy tried and rejected many ideas as she painted. First, she considered setting fire to Vanessa's house, and then going in there on the basis that Vanessa might be in there overcome by smoke. But then suppose the fire got out of hand and destroyed all the evidence? Or got even more out of hand and spread to other houses in the street? Or suppose she got found out and prosecuted for arson; that was a real worry. She'd seen a documentary about arson investigations. They could find out amazing things, it was little short of witchcraft what they could do. No, arson was definitely out.

She considered breaking into Vanessa's house herself, while Vanessa was off at work. But suppose someone saw her get in and called the police? She didn't think Ben would be terribly impressed if his new girlfriend turned out to be a burglar. He'd break up with her for sure. No, burglary was right out.

All they needed was enough to convince the sergeant to get a warrant. It didn't have to be the full shebang. Just one packet of drugs, Tammy supposed, would be enough.

***

It was a hot day, but Tammy shivered as she crouched in the overgrown lilac bushes just inside her front gate. Right, that looked like the car was full. Now was the moment. She pressed the button and let speed dial do the rest. Presently, the shrill of the landline could be faintly heard from inside Vanessa's house. Vanessa, about to close the car door, hesitated, looked back, seemed to deliberate for a second and then hurried back inside.

Tammy didn't lose a second, darting out from the bush and across the road without even looking both ways. Wrenching open the top of the nearest box, she snatched the first thing her groping hand encountered, secured the lid and belted back to the bush just in time to hear Vanessa answer the phone in her pretentious North Shore accent.

'Oh, hi, Vanessa, it's Tammy, from across the road, you know? I was wondering if you could lend me some desiccated coconut. I was going to make a lemon slice and I forgot to get any.' It was the best she'd been able to come up with.

Vanessa's voice drifted to her over the airwaves, sounding just ever so slightly irritated. She did not have any desiccated coconut. A likely story, Tammy thought. Bitch. What kind of Australian woman doesn't have shredded coconut in her pantry? She was more sure than ever that Vanessa was Bad to the Bone. She made her excuses and rang off, scampering up the steps and in through the back door just as Vanessa emerged, got into her Porsche and vroomed off.

Tammy's heart was pounding. She'd always been a daring, innovative thinker, at least that was what her thesis advisor had said, but she'd seldom translated this quality into direct, external, Schwarzenegger-type action. This had been a first, she realised, examining what she held in her hand with mounting excitement. It was a small packet of white powder.

***

'You did WHAT?'

'It was easy, Ben, she even left the car door open. So is it the right stuff?'

The little cellophane packet sat between them on Tammy's kitchen table, seeming to give out a malevolent aura. Ben shook his head. 'I'm going out with Arnold Schwarzenegger.' He sighed, picked up the packet and opened it. He sniffed, very cautiously, at it, then inserted the tip of one finger to pick up a few grains of the powder and rubbed it between his fingers. He closed the packet, and got up to wash his hands at the kitchen sink.

'Looks like it, as far as I can tell. Of course, it'll have to go to the lab to make sure, and you need the lab report for evidence anyway, but this is enough to get a warrant with. But listen here, Tammy, you'd have to give evidence at trial of how you got this, and that just isn't a good idea. These are some very powerful, nasty people you're messing with. I'm not at all happy that you went charging in and did this off your own bat.'

'Why, I've got the results right there in front of you.'

Ben sighed again, a long, mournful sigh that spoke volumes about the inability of the lay person to understand police matters. 'Look, you send some crim away for a good long stretch. But sooner or later, they get out, right? And in the meantime, they've got friends and associates, right? I don't want to come home and find you murdered one dark night.'

Come home? COME HOME? OMG OMG

OMG, shrieked Tammy's mind. OMG he's thinking about... Focus, you silly cow, she told herself. Sternly she forced her mind back to the issue at hand.

'But why me? I wouldn't be the one arresting her. If anyone was going to be murdered one dark night, it'd be you.'

'You're forgetting the trial. That would have to come out in evidence. You'd be on the witness stand and everything.'

Tammy thought for a few seconds.

'Damn. I don't know if I'd make a very good witness, Ben. My memory isn't so good sometimes. I mean, look at now, I completely misremembered about that packet of stuff.'

'What?'

'Yes! It's all coming back to me now. The packet fell out of the box when she was putting it in the car, and I noticed it when I was looking out the window. That was what reminded me I didn't have any coconut, seeing that packet of white stuff, so I rang her to see if I could borrow some. Then I forgot all about the packet she'd dropped, and she drove off, and then you came over and noticed the packet on the ground in her driveway and picked it up.'

'Jesus, Tammy, you can't just rewrite the facts like that.'

'Why not? In fact, now I come to think about it, that's wrong too. I never even saw the packet. You just happened to see it in her driveway, didn't you? Nothing to do with me.'

***

The police raid was better than a movie. Tammy watched from her French windows as police descended on the McMansion from all directions. It took until nearly midnight for it all to be over, as police were coming and going for hours carrying boxes of stuff and pieces of equipment, but far and away the best part was seeing Vanessa led out by Ben and his friend Joel, spitting and screaming like a fishwife, one shoe off, her hair coming down and all her elegance and annoying perfection flung to the winds.

***

Following the arrest and conviction of Vanessa Carlson in a blaze of tabloid publicity, Ben was the hero of the hour. He was commended by the Police Commissioner, and more importantly, returned to ordinary detective duties.

Tom was deemed unfit for further police work as a result of his brush with drugs. Tammy could never see any difference in him, but Dr Wright, the vet, had given Ben a written statement expressing his medical opinion that his constitution was damaged and that he should be immediately retired from active police duty. He and Ben moved into Tammy's house, in order to provide Tom, Ben said, with a settled home environment.

Tammy, of course, received no public recognition for her part in shutting down the Yarrangong drug ring, but the Yarrangong CIB threw a massive party in her honour, at which she was given honorary membership in the detective squad. For a while she toyed with the idea of joining the police force, but Ben's reminiscences of life in the Police Academy, which apparently involved a lot of getting up at dawn and running for miles, soon had her deciding in favour of writing crime novels instead. She found a great satisfaction in constructing almost-perfect crimes, and if her detective hero bore more than a passing resemblance to a certain Detective Senior Constable, her new friends at the station were too kind to remark upon it, at least in her hearing.

# Operation Camilla

# ଚOPERATION CAMILLAଓ

## ଚCHAPTER ONEଓ

Donald Blackman howled with outrage as the dog squatted right in the middle of his new false grass lawn. Dropping his mail and paper, he ran across the grass and aimed a kick at the beast. The big yellow dog evaded the kick, dancing just out of range, pink tongue flapping from the side of its mouth. Blackman lost his balance, skidded on the wet grass and sat heavily on his bottom. He looked quickly about to see if anyone had observed him, but the early morning street, thank God, was quiet and empty. He picked up his slightly mangled newspaper and brandished it at the dog. The dog barked once, dropped low in front in what

Blackman interpreted as mockery, then lifted its head as if hearing a distant call, turned and trotted away.

Blackman strode across his front lawn, plucking damp trousers away from his bottom. Something squelched beneath his foot, and he looked down and roared with rage, scrubbing his foot on the artificial grass and smearing the fresh dog poo more thoroughly over his suede desert boots. Seven o'clock and he could already feel the day slipping out of his grasp, sinking into the vast, amorphous expanse of wasted days that had become his life. He let himself into his semi-detached office and tossed the day's mail and the soggy paper onto his secretary's desk.

In the sanctum of his inner office, he threw himself into his chair and glowered out the window. The day stretched ahead, void of client meetings, void of court appearances, void, if he were honest with himself, of work. The only files he had that were current were a couple of conveyancing matters. He had had to refer most of his regular clients to other practitioners following his trouble, when his practising certificate had been suspended for three months. None of them had come back when he'd reopened his doors. Not a single one. He was relying on his mates at Acme Real Estate for a trickle of conveyancing referrals, but they didn't even generate enough income to cover his secretary's wages.

A few nice, juicy divorces, that was what he needed. High net worth individuals meant rich pickings for the family lawyer. High net worth individuals with children, he mused. Those were the best; the arguments about custody and access could drag on for years, with many court appearances. The nastier it got, the more he raked in.

He heaved his bulk out of the chair, stumped back out to the front office and picked up his newspaper, his mind filled with dreams of golden wealth furnished by human misery. If only, he thought, there were some way to *make* people get divorced.

That prat John Mills was on the front page again, accepting some award. Smug bastard. Businessman of the year. Look at him with his bloody trophy wife and his five blond children. *I'd like to have you in my office fighting for your life, you smarmy git. You wouldn't look so bloody pleased with yourself then.*

He frowned suddenly, bending over the paper to look more closely at the photograph. That wasn't the woman he'd seen Mills with at the Commercial Club last week. She was blonde and uptight-looking. The woman he'd seen last week had been a slutty-looking brunette, with tits the size of watermelons and a skirt that looked like it had been sprayed on. Heh, heh. So Mills was playing away, was he? Dirty bastard. He chuckled appreciatively.

There was nothing much of interest in the paper. Blackman skimmed through it, sneering at the picture of the happy children who'd found their lost dog and the one of the stupid hippy festival. The hippies were no good. They lived on their commune, didn't own enough to bother making wills, and there were never any family law matters; they didn't bloody get married in the first place, and they never seemed to argue over their children even if they did split up. You might get the odd criminal matter – marijuana and the like – but that wasn't worth anything; they were always on Legal Aid, so you could only charge the scheduled fee. Someone like that Mills, that was what you wanted. An enormous asset pool with that thriving department store, probably a self-managed superannuation fund, big expensive house, probably a holiday house too. And plenty at stake, with the five kids. Yes, if only Mills were getting a divorce. If that uptight bitch ever found out about the other woman… He drifted into a pleasant reverie, where a now-humble Mills shivered in the client chair, begging for his help. Allegations of child abuse would make it go on even longer. Sometimes, if you were lucky… of course, a discreet rumour might spark such allegations. As long as it wasn't traceable…

He looked up with a frown as he heard the outer door. 'That you, Shelley?' he called.

'Yes, Mr Blackman.'

Blackman glanced at his watch. It was eight fifteen. 'Get in here,' he roared. 'Now!'

His secretary crept into the office.

'What bloody time do you call this? Hey? Hey?'

'I'm sorry, Mr–'

'Your hours are eight to five. That means you are here at eight every morning. Not swanning in halfway through the morning. DO YOU UNDERSTAND THAT?'

'Yes, Mr Blackman, I'm sor–'

'So what the hell d'you think you're doing turning up at eight fifteen?'

'I'm really sorry, I–'

'Do you think that because you're only nineteen you're not expected to do a full job? Is that it? Think you can just loaf around and come in when it suits you?'

'No, Mr Black–'

'It's not acceptable, Shelley. I pay you to be here and I expect you to be here, on time, every day. Your work's shit, I left the Mulgrave file on your desk, the whole thing has to be retyped. If you paid a bit more attention to your work perhaps you'd be able to do a simple task without having to redo it five times. What kind of impression do you think it makes when you spell the client's name wrong, hey? You stupid little bitch. Do you want to make me look like a fucking amateur? And you need to smarten yourself up, for Christ's sake, you look as if you've been dragged through a fucking hedge.'

She was crying now, he saw with satisfaction, doing her best to hide it but he could see the telltale shine in her eyes, and hear the muffled sniffs. Good; serve her right.

'Get me a coffee,' he snapped. 'At least that's something you can do properly.'

He was engrossed in the paper again when she came back out, carrying a tall porcelain mug. She set it carefully on the corner of the rosewood desk, sliding a coaster under it as she'd learned to do when he'd stopped her wages to pay for its refinishing.

'What's the matter, Shel?' His tone now was kindly, avuncular. Keep them off balance, that was what you did. They worked twice as hard that way, and besides, it was fun. 'Boyfriend playing you up? Sit down and tell me about it. Get yourself a coffee, too.' She flinched as if he'd pointed a gun at her head. 'Ah, come on, Shel, you don't want to pay too much attention when I go off at you. Come on, get yourself a cuppa and sit down.'

Over coffee, employing the client interview skills he'd honed over thirty years of legal practice, he elicited the information that Shelley's boyfriend had dumped her the previous evening. Pleased with this information, Blackman probed further, encouraging her to tell the full story of the relationship.

She'd met him through an online dating agency, it turned out. Blackman pressed his lips together to repress a snigger. They had gone out for dinner and to films a few times, and had slept together after their fifth date. Blackman bit back a yawn. The crisis had come last night, after she'd been seeing him for three months. He had taken her to a really flash restaurant, and it had all been so romantic, blah blah blah… She'd thought he was working up to propose, and then when she went back to his place... At this point Shelley broke down in helpless sobs.

Blackman was bored with the story and wanted to get back to his own work, such as it was, but he felt that as he'd invested nearly half an hour, it ought not to be a total waste. Whatever had prompted the breakup would be a major trigger for the girl, which could be subtly played on for his amusement and profit. So he made sympathetic tut-tutting noises, fetched tissues and a glass of water, and generally behaved like a kindly old uncle. It was good to keep his hand in at this crap anyway; family law clients often needed a lot of sympathy, especially the women.

Patience paid off when she finally finished snuffling and snorting. And what a payoff! Blackman had to hold his breath for twenty seconds so as not to burst out laughing. Instead of the engagement ring the silly bitch had expected, waiting for her in her boyfriend's bedroom had been a leash and collar, and a whip! When she'd demurred, he'd taken the moral high ground by reminding her that her profile on the dating website had said she liked to try new things. Even better, she'd apparently tried to go along with it, but had evidently failed to perform satisfactorily as a dog, and had broken down completely when he demanded that she eat food out of a dog bowl on the floor. Now she felt used, she felt dirty, blah blah blah.

Blackman could no longer restrain himself, and dissolved into giggles that felt unmanly, but were unstoppable. He sat jiggling in his chair, tears of laughter rolling down his face, gesturing helplessly with one hand. After a shocked gasp, the girl resumed howling and fled into the lavatory. The sound of her sobs cut off abruptly as the soundproofed door closed behind her. Blackman subsided into chuckles as he opened the McAllister file. Lead and collar, he murmured to himself, shaking his head. Yarralove.com. God almighty.

***

Tammy sighed as she booted up her computer. Writing a novel was turning out to be a lot more work than she'd imagined, and a lot less fun. She'd been at it for three months now, and it was turning out to be rather a slog. After she'd been instrumental in Ben's catching that horrible drug dealer, she'd decided she was a natural to write detective fiction, what with her Fine Arts degree and her practical experience, but as it turned out, you needed a lot more than a good idea and knowing your way around Proust. She'd got off to a good start, with the basic book drafted in six weeks, but when she had read through it, she'd been horribly disappointed. Not only did it not read well, but it was far too short for a full-length novel. Now she was adding another skin to the onion, layering in subplots and character exposition, and her initial enthusiasm had waned to the point where, some days, she didn't even look at it. The worst of it was that the book seemed to have swallowed up her whole life. She hadn't done any more work on her awful fixer-upper house since she'd started writing it, and it had been a whole three months now. She hadn't even finished the sitting room; it was painted, but that was all, and her bedroom, where she now sat, was furnished only with a mattress on the floor and a still-packed cardboard box to hold her alarm clock, besides, of course, the cheap card table and folding chair where she was presently sitting. Perhaps it was her surroundings that were the problem.

She let her eyes glaze over, forgetting the unfinished book as she thought about how she'd like her bedroom to be. All white would be lovely and peaceful. She'd buy some paint on Saturday, she decided. Having done the sitting room, painting was one thing she really knew how to do. And paint was cheap, unlike furniture and curtains. She certainly had enough cash to buy a big tin of white and some primer. She could move her makeshift bed into the second bedroom while she did it, and that would keep Tom away from the work too; she didn't need black fur floating through the air and sticking to wet paint. Perhaps she could get Ben to help? It was such a couples thing to do, painting a room together. But he was leaving on Sunday night to go on that computer crime course, and would be away for three weeks, so if she wanted him to help, she wouldn't be able to get started until after that. Tammy liked to get on with things as soon as she thought of them. She could have it all finished, easily, by the time Ben got back, and the mattress moved back in. Perhaps she could paint the floor white, too. Could you get paint for floors? Well, she would start with the walls and think about that later.

## ଃCHAPTER TWOଖ

Blackman arrived back at his office at half past three, feeling mellow after a bottle and a half of Cabernet Sauvignon. He had told the story about Shelley's boyfriend to three of his cronies at the Commercial Club, to roars of laughter. No doubt it would get about, but what the hell – she was a miserable whiny bitch anyway, and he didn't suppose it would make a lot of difference to her constant snivelling.

That wasn't the best thing, though, although he'd had a fine time at lunch. The best thing was the idea he'd had as he was driving unsteadily back from the club. The idea that would rejuvenate his ailing practice. The idea that would generate family law matters, and more family law matters, pretty much, as far as he could see, on demand.

Ignoring the still-weepy Shelley hunched over her desk, he went into his office and closed the door. Pressing the intercom button on his phone, he barked, 'No calls this afternoon.' He settled back in his chair, crossed his hands over his stomach and stared at the ceiling. There were a number of details to be worked out.

First and foremost, of course, he would need a computer expert. The degree of computer skill necessary to this project was, he knew, far beyond him. He knew where to get one, though. His nephew, Josh, had graduated from RMIT last year, and was now working at PCs R Us, just three doors down from the Commercial Club. With the right cover story, he might not even need to pay him.

That would take a bit of thought, though. Josh was a smart boy, very smart, and it would take something special to get him to work free. Something idealistic, he thought. All these young kids were all about saving the planet, and all that goody-goody rubbish. But at the same time it had to be *cool*. That was what young people cared about. Being cool. He gazed around his messy, cluttered office, looking for inspiration. His eye fell on the paperback he was reading. Ah yes, now he had it. That would get him. He reached for the telephone.

***

Ben leaned back in his chair, letting out a sigh of satisfaction. 'Ahhhh. Best thing I ever did, moving in here. You keep this up, you minx, I'm gonna have to spend every night in the gym.'

Tammy eyed him fondly. He certainly could eat for England. How nice it was to have someone demanding third helpings every night. Ben's uncritical appetite made her feel like Nigella Lawson. 'I don't think you're putting on weight, Ben. You look great to me.'

They enjoyed a sappy moment. Then Tammy rose to start on the dishes. 'Haven't you got packing to do?'

'Shit, yeah.' He leaped up. 'Nearly forgot. Shit, three whole weeks. I'm going to miss you, Tam. And your cooking. And you, you little scoundrel.' He bent to lift Tom to his shoulder. 'You won't forget to worm him, will you, Tammy? It's due on Friday.'

'No, Ben, I won't forget to worm him. And I won't forget to feed him. And I won't forget to give him cuddles. Go on, get out of here.' She flicked the dish towel at him as he exited the kitchen, Tom draped around his neck like a black fur scarf.

***

'… a matter of national security.'

Josh regarded his uncle sceptically. 'Seems odd they don't have their own computer people, though. I mean, a big organisation like Asio.'

Blackman tapped the side of his nose. 'It's a black op, Josh. Full freedom, but no support. I'm on my own with this. And I need the help of someone I can trust. I need your help, Josh. For the children,' he finished, with a significant look.

'Children? What children?'

Damn, he'd laid it on too thick. 'Figure of speech, mate. I mean the security of our nation, and the country our children are going to inherit, see what I mean?'

'Alright, Uncle Don. What was it you wanted me to do?'

'I need you to hack into a website. This website.' He passed over a slip of paper. 'I want to know everyone they have dealings with.'

Josh stared at the paper. 'Uncle Don, I know this site. It's a dating agency.'

'Ostensibly. Huh? Huh?' He waggled his eyebrows in what he hoped was a meaningful way.

'I want to know everyone who's on their list, and the codenames they're using. If you can get copies of their communications in and out, that would be ideal.'

'But Uncle Don, a dating agency?'

'Think about it, Josh. Communications going in and out all the time. People using code names. Meetings being arranged. Think about it. We want to know where and when those meetings are taking place.'

He had him now. The kid's eyes were shining.

'Can you do it, Josh? Remember, no risks. I may risk my own life for my country, but yours is not on the table.'

'Let me see what I can do, 'kay?'

'And no talking about it on the phone. If you see me anywhere but here, don't say anything. This room's been swept for bugs, but…'

Josh nodded. 'Say no more, Uncle Don. My lips are sealed.' He made a zipping gesture across his mouth.

'We'll meet back here in, say, a week. If anyone asks, I was having some trouble with my computer. Everyone knows I'm a technophobe. It's useful for them to know that, if you know what I mean.'

'Geez. Do you have, like, a Batcave under here?'

Good lord. The boy was even younger than he looked. Blackman did his best to paste a mysterious expression on his face. 'Need to know basis, Josh, capisce?'

***

Tammy hummed happily to herself as she sanded. She'd set herself up as usual with her headphones and an audiobook, but had found her attention drifting away from it as her thoughts returned, again and again, to her own book and its problems. After half an hour she'd tossed the headphones aside. The mindless, monotonous physical work seemed to activate her writer's brain, and as she worked, plot glitches sorted themselves out and opportunities for character development occurred to her. She decided to add a romance subplot as her thoughts drifted to Ben, now boarding his flight to Melbourne. Her detective protagonist was modelled on him, although of course she'd had to make him rather more clever. Ben wasn't… well, he was lovely, and beautiful-looking, and endlessly good-natured, but he probably, she thought, wasn't the sharpest tool in the box. It didn't matter to her. You didn't need everyone to be clever. Neville, her ex-husband, had been as brainy as they came, and look at him. The prick. Ben had better not ever play around. She'd report him to the internal affairs office. The police still had an internal offence of Moral Turpitude, Ben had told her. What a great word 'turpitude' was.

All the same, she mused as she wrapped a fresh sheet of sandpaper around the block, it would be nice if Ben could share some of the more intellectual of her interests. He never seemed to have read anything she mentioned, and, now she came to think of it, she didn't think she'd ever seen him with a book in his hand. And when he'd moved in, he'd unpacked his clothes and personal stuff, and kitchen gear, but there hadn't been the boxes of books she'd expected.

She pushed away a guilty thought of the pile of boxes still stacked in the back bedroom. What was the point of unpacking them anyway, when she didn't have any bookshelves? Perhaps she should have looked at furniture first, instead of all this painting. But then she'd have to move it all to paint. She shuddered at the memory of the one time she'd rearranged her living room. No, once a bookcase was in place it needed to stay there. Forever.

Anyway, you couldn't do everything at once. Get this room painted, so it would be all nice and fresh when Ben came home. And finish the book, those were her priorities. Everything else could wait…

*** 

Josh worked steadily, headphones pumping a blast of rock music straight into his mind. He was already into the Yarralove site, and had downloaded their client database. It had been a stroke of luck that they used cloud storage for their admin system. He wondered how many of these losers were actually spies. Maybe Uncle Don would recruit him to do some real espionage work, in person. He wouldn't mind matching wits with some of those women. Phwoarrrrr…

The site offered a service that allowed members to arrange their first meeting anonymously, using only their designated nicknames. Josh was a bit surprised at this; if he was going to hook up with some woman he met online, he'd want to talk to her first, at least chat on the phone before he committed himself to a full-on date. What if she was a moron? Still, he supposed these people weren't in it to find life partners. It was all too apparent what they were in it for, just by the information they entered on their profiles. 'Love new and exciting experiences…', 'looking to share', whatever that meant. He shuddered to think, especially after looking at the photograph that went with that one. 'Humble slave looking for a master' – yuk. 'Likes it doggie style'– okaaaay. 'Enjoys risk-taking'. 'Likes brown showers'. Josh stopped at that one. Surely no one cared *that* much about bathroom décor? He took a minute to google the phrase, then wished he hadn't. These people were all perverts. Josh liked to think he was as open-minded as the next person, but some things were just… he hoped the brown shower guy was one of the spies.

The downloaded data were in an Access database, and it didn't take long at all to generate a few reports. One master list linking codename, real name, email address, billing address, age and credit card number. Josh didn't really see the relevance of the credit card number, but it looked weak just to have names and addresses, so he added this, and also gender and gender sought, and then a freeform text field to contain the variable-length descriptions people had provided. These were the ones mentioning things like 'brown shower' and 'looking for a master'. Josh set up the report to output into an Excel spreadsheet, rather than print. He didn't think Uncle Don would be printing anything out, for security reasons.

He generated another listing containing cross-references between each member and those members with whom they had hooked up. Perhaps there would be patterns Uncle Don would find useful. A third listing, of enormous size, dumped out all the messages that members had sent each other via the Yarralove website. All three reports went onto a USB stick. Then, feeling something was lacking, he reran the main report and included thumbnail photographs.

Job done, he hesitated for a moment. The database was fun to play with, and perhaps Uncle Don would ask for something he hadn't thought of. But Uncle Don had been very clear about the need to leave no traces. He copied it, however, onto another USB stick, of larger capacity than the ones he kept to trade with his friends, and slipped it between the covers of his battered copy of Lord of the Rings. Then he deleted all the files he had created on his hard drive and, for good measure, started a defrag, with initialisation, to erase any traces. Another time, he thought, it would be better to do the whole download onto an external hard drive, of which he had several; the drive could be formatted afterwards for maximum safety.

Blackman was delighted with the results of his nephew's hacking operation, and paid him $100 for his trouble, and a further $50 to set him up with a free, untraceable email account and website hosting. Once the boy had left, he settled down to plan his next move.

# CHAPTER THREE

**B**lackman groaned in frustration. He had been at it for six hours, and his new website, godhateswhores.com, still looked like shit. The free hosting service provided an easy-to-use template, or so it claimed, but easy-to-use for most people didn't seem to mean easy-to-use for a middle-aged solicitor who still used a Dictaphone and got a secretary to type everything. He wished he could just dump the job on Shelley and shout at her when it wasn't up to the standard he wanted, as he ordinarily did with anything involving technology. He had had to resort to barring her from his office and telling her to reorganise the filing cabinets, which were located in the outer office. At least she wasn't enjoying her day any more than he was; the hanging files were stuffed past capacity, and the outer rims of the hanging bits had sharp edges.

When he'd come back from lunch, her fingers had been covered in band-aids, and he'd shouted at her for looking sloppy, and ordered her to get rid of them, which had relieved his stress even more than Beef Wellington and half a bottle of Cabernet Sauvignon.

The website was modelled on that of the Westboro Baptist Church, with an ostensible focus on Public Morality. He'd even copied a number of articles from that well-known site, altering them as needed to replace their obsession with homosexuals with one with chastity. There needed to be plenty of content, to make it look real. He surfed the web for more extreme right-wing religious content, plagiarising freely since the whole thing was anonymous anyway. For variety, he added a number of racial hatred articles, concentrating particularly on refugees and Stop The Boats rhetoric, of which he found plenty. He mixed these in with his morality content and backdated everything to make it look as though the website had been around for a while. By the time he stopped work at seven, he had a basic website that he thought might be believable. He would sleep on it and look at it again in the morning before deciding to hit the Publish button, which Josh had explained would make the website visible to everyone on the web.

***

Tammy had not slept well, despite having got up super-early the previous day to see Ben off on his plane, spent the day setting up her painting project, and then worked an exhausting night shift at the supermarket. The second bedroom, where she'd dragged her mattress after Ben had left, was all wrong; the light came from the wrong side, and there wasn't enough of it, as the front room faced north, and she kept half-waking all morning. Most of all, though, the double mattress was horribly empty with just her and Tom. Tom was a comfort, of course, and she had finally managed to get to sleep, burying her face in his black fur and listening as his rumbling purr gave way to scratchy little snores. He was gone when she awoke, out the makeshift cat door in the front door (she really must get that pane replaced) and away on whatever cat business called him out each afternoon.

Yawning, she dragged on her working clothes (disreputable, saggy tracksuit pants and an old football jersey), made herself a cup of tea and resumed sanding. She was halfway around the room now, having finally stopped when the need to write down the ideas she'd come up with for her flagging novel had reached a level of pressure that she couldn't withstand. Now, a comprehensive set of notes outlining two subplots and various character-developing incidents was safely in her notebook.

For a moment, she was tempted to make that the day's job, but Ben was due back in three weeks' time, and the bedroom painting was going to be his surprise, and that was that.

It was lucky, Tammy thought, that the walls in this room were in fairly good repair. She wouldn't need to be plastering over cracks, and resanding, and all of that. Perhaps the bedrooms hadn't had much use; from the state of the living room when she'd moved in, it could reasonably be inferred that no one had ever remained sober enough to be able to find their way to a bed. Her first week in the house had been entirely consumed in scrubbing every available surface with Domestos, and then tea tree oil, to get rid of the pervasive stench of urine, vomit and marijuana. She still caught whiffs of tea tree whenever she opened a cupboard.

*** 

On the other side of Yarrangong, in the posh part of town, up on the hill, Donald Blackman, barrister and solicitor, as the brass plate next to his office door announced, was at his creative work again. He had published his website, and was now working on a new version. You could work on it all you wanted, Josh had explained, but the public would only see the results of your changes once you hit 'Publish' again.

Blackman was creating sub-pages. He had selected from the client list, which he had printed off on the office printer once Shelley had gone home, the names of two of the wealthiest and most influential citizens of Yarrangong. One of them was, in fact, the mayor. His preferences evidently ran to young women of a different racial heritage. Very young women, very young indeed. Although, Blackman mused, Asian women often did look far younger than they were. He wondered if they looked young to everyone, or only to Europeans. Anyway, it didn't matter; the point was that Mayor Polk was a married man and a pillar of the Methodist church. Heh heh.

The other man Blackman had selected to be one of his first victims was John Mills, purely on the basis that he resented Mills for being smug, for being chosen Yarrangong Businessman of the Year, for having a later model Porsche than his, Blackman's, and for having that sickeningly perfect family. Blackman's own wife had left him some years before, saying that she was sick of his rudeness, sick of his abuse, sick of his drunken friends and sick of him generally. They had had no children.

Each page was headed with a photograph of the victim. Instead of using the ones supplied to Yarralove, he had downloaded photographs from the website of the Yarrangong Times. The one of the mayor showed him in his full mayoral regalia at some public event with his wife. The one of Mills, of course, was the photograph that had recently been printed, of him receiving the Yarrangong Businessman of the Year award, with his blonde wife and five tow-headed children.

Text below the pictures outed each man as an adulterer, and revealed the details of their membership in Yarralove, providing their credit card numbers as evidence and giving details of the dates they had joined the dating service. In the case of Mills, his appearance at the Commercial Club was also detailed, and the photograph of the woman, whom Blackman had been able to identify from the database, was also displayed, along with her name and credit card number. 'CAUGHT IN THE ACT' was the page's headline. It had taken Blackman three quarters of an hour to work out how to make it display in big red letters, but it was worth it, he reckoned. He added a big red title to the mayor's page, too. 'DO YOU WANT THIS MAN RUNNING YOUR TOWN?' it said.

He added an article to the main page decrying the breakdown of the sanctity of the marriage bond in modern Australia, and clicked on the 'Publish' button with a satisfaction he hadn't experienced since he'd successfully stripped a client's husband of his entire superannuation entitlement. The only thing that could have made it better would have been if Mills had been the 'brown showers' guy. Blackman had looked it up on Google, and part of him felt rather sick, even as the other part chortled at the damage it could do in a custody battle. The bloke seemed to be a nobody, though. He might do down the track, if he was married (he had not specified his marital status), but Blackman was after the rich pickings he could get from high net worth individuals.

Now to ensure that the right people saw it. Blackman had given this careful thought. He didn't want to be too direct. It would be best if someone else, some real person, was the one to bring it to the attention of the victims' wives.

He started by creating a Facebook account in a generic name. He uploaded a random picture of a fluffy cat as the profile picture. Josh had explained all this. Apparently it was quite usual for young women to use pictures of animals instead of their own pictures. Now to get some friends, so as to look like a real person. Join some groups, Josh had said. Since he was already using a cat as his profile picture, he typed 'cat' into the search box. There was an interest, so he 'liked' that, and joined something called Family Share. He applied to join a group called 'Cat Lovers', one called 'Black Cats

Rock', and one called 'Jellicle Cats'. He hastily found a picture of a black cat and made that his profile picture instead, to justify his interest. Pretty soon his membership application to Cat Lovers was approved. He surfed about, liked some cat pages and shared some pictures of cats to fill up his timeline. He liked some bible study pages as well. Getting some friends would be the trick. He knew he needed to do that, and quickly, or he was just not going to look real. Then, biting the bullet, he entered random strings in the search field and sent friend requests to half a dozen people. God knew why anyone would accept a friend request from a total stranger, but Josh had said people did it all the time. He logged out, locked up his office and went through the connecting door into the house.

***

By the time she had to leave for work, Tammy was depressed. Dinner for one was no novelty; Ben, a police detective, worked varying shifts. But having dinner alone when your partner was just a phone call away and would be home at 11:30 was one thing, and having dinner alone when he was hundreds of miles away and wouldn't be home for three weeks was quite another. Just to put the icing on the cake, Tom hadn't come home from his morning jaunt. It was nothing to worry about, she told herself. Tomcats did roam. Tom could look after himself. Still, it had been a sad little meal, and she'd left half of the lasagne she'd microwaved. She scraped out some of the meat filling onto the top of Tom's untouched dinner. He'd enjoy it when he got home.

Tammy's shift at the supermarket started at ten p.m., when the store closed to customers. For the next six hours she would stock shelves, the monotonous work relieved only by the frequent smoke breaks called by her fellow workers, none of whom could be called exactly dedicated. Tammy often wondered how many people it would take to work the night shift if everyone just buckled down and worked, instead of mucking about. But it was easy work, they were a friendly bunch, and it didn't take anything from your brain. She generally listened to an audiobook through most of her shift, so it was almost like leisure time, with gentle exercise. She turned out the lights and locked the door. Tom would get in through the broken pane at the bottom. She really must get that fixed. It had been broken during her rental tenancy, before settlement had taken place, so it should have been fixed by the vendor as landlord, but despite many promises he had never turned up. Anyway, it was useful for Tom, saving her the expense and trouble of a catflap. She didn't make much from her supermarket job, and although things had eased when Ben had moved in and started sharing expenses, she still had to be careful, always mindful of the possibility of a major expense with her old banger of a car.

# CHAPTER FOUR

Once a few people had accepted his friend request, Blackman sent requests to a few more, selecting people who were already friends with his existing friends. Each time he sent ten or so requests, there would usually be at least one person who accepted. In this way he got up to a respectable twenty-seven friends over the course of a week. Then he started to search for people living in the local area. This was a bit more risky, as he was a fictional entity, and people might well expect actually to know him, but he had chosen one of the surnames that belonged to an enormous extended family; Yarrangong was full of Somervilles; they were, so to speak, legion. Therefore for any given Somerville, he reasoned, it would be quite on the cards that one might know them without really knowing them. The name itself was almost a kind of bona fide passport.

By the end of the second week, he had acquired fifty-six friends in and around Yarrangong. He was ready for Phase Two. He set up another fictitious Facebook account, in the name of Frank Phillips; this was the name he had used on the website as the webmaster.

Cursing at his oversight in not having started the process before, he quickly joined every extreme right-wing page he could find, and sent friend requests to the most egregiously rednecked posters in those groups. This time, it took a mere three days to get to a hundred facebook friends, and it was more fun, too. He quite enjoyed letting loose with the most racist, homophobic remarks he could think of.

Thus prepared, he created a Facebook page for his false organisation and filled it with posts copied at random from similar websites to his own. Then he shared the page and waited for his new, racist, homophobic friends to like it. Response to this exceeded his wildest hopes, with twenty-three shares and seventy-eight likes in the first two hours. Finally, relying on the fabled 'six degrees of separation', he logged in as Judy Somerville, located his new page and the link to Mayor Polk's page on the website, and shared it publicly, with a message consisting chiefly of 'OMG!!!!!!' and 'he should sue them'.

***

Tammy had not been sleeping well, or eating well, or really doing anything very well since Ben had left for his course. It wasn't so much that she was missing him, she told herself. Not pining or anything like that. Certainly not. It was more that she was starting to wonder, now that he was away, if it had really been wise letting him move in here. Hadn't they, she wondered, rushed things just a tiny bit? They had only been seeing each other for a few weeks at the time.

Mind you, she'd been keen enough; it wasn't as if Ben had talked her into anything. Right from the start they'd hit it off like cheese and olives. But hadn't it all been a bit, well, too easy? They'd met, bam, they'd started dating, bam bam, they'd slept together, triple bam with bells and whistles and catherine wheels, but where, she asked herself, where had been the soul-searching? The angst? The drunken, tortured self-revelatory phone calls to her girlfriends at four in the morning? The tears, for heaven's sake. These things went with love, Tammy knew, as smoke went with fire. So didn't that mean that she and Ben were not really a match made in heaven, despite their apparent total compatibility, despite their extreme lust for each other, despite the fact they'd never spoken a cross word in four months of living together, despite the fact they enjoyed the same food, the same movies, even the same dance styles?

All through those solitary weeks, as Tammy scrubbed her bedroom walls with Domestos, as she spread a thick coat of undercoat, as she layered on the first coat and topcoat, she struggled against a growing conviction that she ought to break up with Ben.

*** 

Donald Blackman, barrister-at-law and Officer of the Supreme Court, suffered from no such angst. He whistled cheerily as he strode down the path to unlock his office. When he threw his rolled-up newspaper at the cat that was always hanging about, and which, he was almost certain, was the culprit in regard to the pungent scent on his office door that greeted him every morning, he did it with a smile, and his throw was almost half-hearted.

There had been a big reaction to his inflammatory Facebook post. One hundred and forty-three people had now shared it. He was confident that the news was, even now, trickling its way to its intended targets – the wives of Mayor Polk and John Mills. He tidied his office, and even asked for Shelley's input on making the outer area more attractive.

*****

The news broke the following Wednesday, with headlines in the Yarrangong Times. Blackman was not surprised at the delay, for he knew the paper's editor had sought legal advice before printing the article; he had, in fact, consulted Blackman. Blackman, who didn't really care if the paper was sued, since they were already his clients, had phrased his letter of advice with the greatest care, advising that he didn't think it was likely but that there was always a possibility of litigation arising from any public statement: in essence, saying nothing. He advised the paper to express no opinion on the matter, but report only the facts. That, he felt, covered him against a charge of carelessness or Unsatisfactory Professional Conduct. As he had already gone down on the more serious charge of Professional Misconduct, and had even had his practising certificate suspended for three months, it was vital to avoid any further trouble. He spent an hour and a half on the letter, and charged the newspaper twenty-eight units. As a lawyer's unit is six minutes, this amounted to almost double the time he had actually spent.

For several days, no one in Yarrangong talked about anything else. At the Commercial Club, where Blackman went every day for his lunch, his cronies discussed it endlessly. The consensus was that Polk and Mills had had it coming and that they deserved what they got. The men's disapproval was not so much of the immorality of their conduct as of their stupidity in getting caught. At the barber's, when he went for his haircut, everyone was talking about it. The conversation there centred around sympathy for the betrayed wives, and speculation about whether divorces would be in the offing. Blackman listened and said nothing, for Janet Polk had already engaged him, and Shirley Mills had made an appointment for the following Monday. When asked for his opinion, he contented himself with tutting and shaking his head sadly. 'A dreadful business,' he said, chortling inwardly. This seemed to satisfy everyone, each hearer of the stock remark reading into it agreement with his own position.

***

Tammy, by this time sunk in misery, read the news as she sat in her kitchen, hunched over her morning coffee. She broke down in sobs as she read. Having already had her own life overturned by adultery, she was the ultimate sympathetic audience. Tears rolled down her cheeks as she squinted to make out the increasingly blurry newsprint. At least, she thought, when she'd caught Neville, pants round his ankles, communing with her best friend over the kitchen table, it hadn't been public knowledge. Tom, sitting on the table, stared worriedly, and after a while, stalked over and interposed his body, trampling down the shaking paper and standing on it, turning round and round, rubbing his face on hers, headbutting her with his loud, rumbling purr.

When Ben rang up that night, all happy because he was coming home in two days' time, she almost started crying again as she told him about the story. Ben couldn't understand why she was so upset. 'But you don't even know them,' he kept saying. She hadn't told him anything about the dark thoughts swirling in her mind. It wasn't a subject for the telephone. Serious subjects had to be discussed over the kitchen table, with tea. She started to sniffle again as she imagined talking about this with Ben in that situation. Their kitchen table had always been such a warm and happy place.

On Thursday she got up early, and worked frantically to get the last of the trim painted, so the paint smell could air out before Ben got home on Friday night. He had booked a late flight rather than staying the extra night, although he'd raved about how much he was enjoying the luxury accommodation. The hotel had a big swimming pool and a gym. There was a sauna and a spa, and twenty-four channels on the television. Ben, who had grown up in a poor family, and was a country boy through and through, revelled in it all. He'd been having saunas early every morning, steaming out the effects of drinking in the bar with the other police on the course. The course itself, according to Ben, had been deeply technical, and almost impossible to understand. 'I can't see the point of it,' he had said. 'You don't get computer crime in the country. It's a city thing.'

***

On Monday, the next story hit the stands. Two more local men and one woman were outed as clients of the agency.

Blackman, in his office, fumed and ground his teeth. He had put the pages up on the website at two hour intervals on Friday afternoon, and had been hoping it would make the big Saturday issue of the Yarrangong Times. The circulation of the Saturday paper was more than double that of the weekday editions. Still, he supposed it didn't matter in the long run. The woman, although single, was a teacher at one of the high schools, and had described herself as 'a connoisseur of a tight butt'. She had already left three messages on the voicemail when Shelley checked it on Monday morning.

Blackman, reading the paper, was in too good a mood to do more than shout cursorily at Shelley for not writing the messages more neatly. He sent her off to the shops to find something to remove the smell of cat piss from his front door, and settled down to enjoy the story, which this time had rated a double page spread, plus the editorial. He had to turn the pages with extreme care, as the paper was once again damp, and smelled rather strongly of what he suspected might be dog piss. In addition, the outer pages were scored through by what looked like claw marks. The dog and cat repelling crystals he had bought to scatter along the edges of his property did not seem to work at all.

*****

Of all the denizens of Yarrangong, Ben was perhaps one of the only ones to be purely happy on that Monday morning. He had had a wonderful time in the city, staying at a flash hotel, going out with his new mates every evening and starting every day with a sauna, followed by a full English breakfast, which he never got at home, Tammy being always fast asleep when he got up for day shift. Despite all this, he was ecstatic to be home. Tammy had already gone to work when he'd got in, so he had failed to notice the transformation of their bedroom, but had wandered around and around the house, too keyed up to sleep, carrying Tom in his arms and marvelling at his good fortune, until he'd heard her key in the door. She had seemed tired, he thought.

Probably she'd been missing him badly. God knew he had missed her. Despite the luxury hotel and the novelty of it all, despite the new friends he'd made, somehow the gloss had been off things.

Day shift for police starts at seven a.m., so Ben had not seen the paper before he presented himself, scrubbed and suited and sharply lemon-scented, at the Yarrangong C.I.B. office. He whistled as he climbed the stairs, and greeted the other detectives with high good humour. Ben was happy to be back on the job. He loved his work, he loved his mates, he even loved his gruff Sergeant. That morning, Ben was full of charity for all the world. When Sergeant Stevenson stuck his head out of his office and summoned him for 'a word', he strolled jauntily across the room, grinning hugely.

# ❧CHAPTER FIVE☙

'**B**en, come in, mate. Take a seat. Good to have you back,' said Sergeant Stevenson, shaking Ben's hand and gesturing towards a chair. He sat down behind his desk and sighed, rubbing his eyes. 'It's just in the bloody nick of time, that's all I can say. I sent you on that computer crime course for a treat, you did so well with the Carlson case that I thought it would be a nice break for you, trip to the city, bit of fun, kind of thing. Just as bloody well I did, that's all. Have you seen the papers at all since you got back?'

The grin died on Ben's face. For the first time, he noticed how worn the sergeant was looking. Even this early in the day, his shirt had a wrinkled, slept-in look, and the bags under his eyes were actual pouches. He shook his head. 'Not really, mate. Just a quiet weekend with – well, you know.'

Stevenson snorted. 'Well, you're it, mate. The one and only expert we've got in this kind of crime. Thank God I sent you on that course instead of the anti-terrorism one.'

Ben had a sinking feeling. A good part of the course had been gibberish to him, and although he'd done his best to keep up, he knew he wasn't the sharpest tool in the box about that kind of thing. He hadn't known all the words the instructor had used, and had been too embarrassed to ask, since everyone else had seemed to know what the bloke was talking about.

'We've got a hacking case on our hands,' the sergeant went on. 'Someone's hacked into the database of that Yarralove mob, and they've been leaking shit all over the shop about local people. Some very prominent citizens are involved. I'm under a lot of pressure to solve this quickly, Ben. A lot of pressure.'

'What Yarralove mob?' asked Ben, who had never heard of it.

'You know, that, well I suppose you call it an introduction agency. You know, lonely hearts kind of stuff. You want a woman, you ring up and they fix you up with one.'

'A brothel?'

'Nah, well, not that they admit, anyhow. It's just the introductions. You look at the profiles, women're in it too, they join, men join, then they pick out someone from the photos and that. You must have seen the ads for it.'

Ben, who had not wanted for female company since he'd been twelve, shook his head.

'Here, I'll show you.' Stevenson typed something into the url bar on his computer and turned the screen around so Ben could see it. A pale pink screen was displayed, with 'Yarralove' across the top in big, curly red letters.

'The owner's given me an admin password, so we can look at everything. See, you log in here,' he suited his actions to his words, 'and then you can browse through what's on offer. These fields here are for narrowing it down. Like, if you're a man looking for women, you select this, and this, or if you're looking for a man, you select that, and so forth. And then you can type words in here and it'll match up on what they've put in about themselves. Say, if they like dogs, or play golf or whatever.'

He clicked on a big red heart, and a row of pictures of women displayed on the screen. Some of them were not wearing very much. Reading the tables below the pictures, Ben saw there were various statistics – age, smoker or non-smoker, occupation, marital status –

'Hang on,' said Ben, shocked. 'Half these women're married. What are they doing in a thing like this?'

The sergeant snorted again. 'That's the least of our worries. Look, I'll give you the papers so you can see what they've done with the information. And here,' he scribbled on a post-it note, 'here's the login and password to get into the site. And the url of the other site.'

'What other site?'

'The one where they're publishing all the shit they've got out of this database.' He bundled up a messy-looking pile of newspapers and handed it over the desk. 'Right, that's everything, I think. Off you go. Try to wrap it up as quickly as you can. You'll see why.' He turned his attention back to the file he had open on his desk. Ben was dismissed.

He made his way back to his desk, feeling lost and hopeless. He could not remember anything at all from his course. He'd left the notebook in which he'd made what notes he could at home, not expecting ever to need it again.

'So, the hero returns,' called Bert Sharpe from his desk, where he was eating a doughnut, getting crumbs all down his front. 'Our very own computer geek. The new head of Operation Camilla.'

'Operation what? What you talking about?'

Sharpe sniggered. 'That's what we've been calling it. On account of, you know, all these high and mighty types being caught screwing around.'

'High and mighty... listen, mate, all I know is apparently someone hacked into this Yarralove mob. If you know something more, now would be a good time to share it.'

'Just what was in the papers. Whole town's been talking about it. What, did you just get back this morning or something?'

Ben could feel the blood rising to his face. He turned away to his desk in a vain attempt to stop Sharpe seeing him blush like a girl.

'Aw-haw-haw! Stud boy's been in bed all weekend. You dirty dog. How is young Tammy, by the way?'

Ben's ears burned as he sat at his desk. He opened the top newspaper and buried his head in it, wincing as he failed to block out the ribald laughter of his two colleagues. They knew and liked Tammy, he reminded himself, they weren't saying anything at which he needed to take offence. It was just... he didn't like it.

Half an hour later, he had a rough idea of the severity of the problem. It was extremely severe. He had no idea whatever how to approach it in a technical way, so fell back on his normal way of working. He went to see the victim.

***

The physical premises of Yarralove.com were not what Ben had expected from the website. They were located up a narrow flight of stairs, above Harry's Café, the primary gathering place of Yarrangong's worst behaved teenagers. Access to the stairs was from the back of the café, in a small, cobbled yard full of overflowing dustbins and unidentifiable smells. The stairs were lit only by faint light from a grimy window on the first floor, and as he stepped on the first step, he had an unpleasant sensation of sticking to the floor. The iron handrail felt damp too, and he had to restrain an impulse to wrap his handkerchief around his hand.

As he climbed, the sounds of pinball machines and the throaty shriek of Harry's espresso machine echoed in the confined space. He could hear water dripping from somewhere, a sad, monotonous drip that sounded like depression and failure.

There were two doors on the landing. The one at the back, Harry had said, was a storeroom for the café. The other was Yarralove.com. There was nothing on the doors to indicate this. Ben squared his shoulders and knocked his loud, confident police knock.

There was no answer to the first knock, so Ben, following police custom, knocked again even louder, without waiting very long. Presently a querulous tone filtered through the door, which, Ben had noted, was an interior door, thin sheets of plywood enclosing empty space. He had known this without even thinking about it, from the sound and sensations of knocking on it. Put your foot through it easily, he thought. Not much security for a business. He couldn't make out the words over the rattle of the pinball machines below; the stairwell seemed to act as a kind of sound funnel, but from the general sound of it he translated it as 'alright, I'm coming, no need to beat the bloody door down.'

Max Panagiotidis ('Don't worry, no one can say it. Call me Max.') was a middle-aged man somewhat below average height. Ben mentally catalogued him as he introduced himself and shook hands. Not exactly fat, but on the pudgy side. Soft roll of fat around the middle. Doesn't work out.

Hair thinning and receding, combed straight back and long around the back and sides. Slicked down with some kind of grease, either that or he doesn't ever wash it. Hasn't shaved this morning. Blue shirt open halfway to the waist. Plenty of chest hair. Christ, he must look like a rug with his shirt off. Brown suit, seen better days, baggy at the knees, some kind of shiny fabric, not wool. Nicotine stains on fingers of right hand. Heavy smoker.

He followed Max through a dim living room, to a grimy kitchen. These are residential premises, he thought.

'Um, I was expecting, well, more of an office. This is Yarralove, right? Where you run the business from?'

'Yeah, that's right.'

'It doesn't look much like a business premises.' Ben made the statement and waited. You got more out of suspects by this technique than by firing off questions.

Max waved a hand. 'Doesn't matter. It's all online, see? There's no clients coming up here. They sign up online, they pay online, everything's online. I gotta have an address to register the business name, that's all. I live here. Computer and that's all in the computer room. Wanna see?'

Ben did want to see. He still cherished a vision of white tiles and gleaming surfaces. He followed Max through a small hallway into what was evidently the flat's second bedroom, where a battered old desk held an ordinary-looking desktop computer and a telephone. A card table to one side of it held a small combination printer/copier/fax.

Max shuffled to the window and pulled the cord to open the venetian blinds slightly. This admitted more light, and a view of a blank brick wall, which looked close enough to touch.

'Reckon I know what you're thinking. Not much to look at, eh?' He stubbed out his cigarette in an ashtray that bore signage from the Commercial Club, and immediately pulled out a crumpled packet. 'Smoke?'

Ben shook his head.

'See, it's not just the customer interface. The whole business is online. Cloud computing, it's called. I pay a monthly fee to the computer mob, and they set it all up. Host the website, store all the data, make backups, the lot. It's the way of the twenty-first century, mate. They do everything. See, if something happens here – you know, the building burns down or something – all I need is any computer with internet access and my access codes, and I can go on running the show from anywhere.

In theory, I could carry on trading with not a day lost, even from an internet café. The only reason the business has a physical address at all is like I said, to register the business name you gotta have it. I even get my bills by email. I pay them online.'

Ben digested this in silence for a moment.

'And the setup was nothing at all. None of that renting premises, getting shopfitters in, purchasing furniture and shit. None of that. Don't need to hire any staff, so there's no payroll to worry about, no employment worries, none of that bullshit. I tell you, mate, the business practically runs itself.'

Ben seized on the one piece of information that seemed relevant.

'So, you don't employ anyone at all?'

'Not a soul. It's just me.'

'Did you ever employ anyone, before you got on this cloud thing?'

'Nuh. Started the whole thing from scratch.' He beamed with pride. 'All my own work. My brainchild, you might say.'

Ben's first thought, which had been that most workplace sabotage is committed by disgruntled former employees, died. His second thought rose in its place.

'So how much, roughly, would you say this newspaper business has cost you? In terms of lost income, kind of thing.'

'Jesus, mate, just ask me how much I make a fucking year, why don't you? Cause it comes to about the same thing. It's dead, mate, dead in the water. Ever since this happened, since that first article in the paper, I might as well have shut down.'

'So it's costing you a fair bit, then. Will your insurance cover it?'

Max snorted. 'Maybe if I had any. When I started up, the rates was too high. See, they want to see a couple of years' trading figures to estimate the amount of loss if something happens, and I didn't have that, and then with being in the cloud, see, I didn't think it was worthwhile anyway. Fire, flood, anything like that, see, I could cope with it. I never bargained on anything like this happening. I mean, who'd do it? Who? Bloody bible-bashers. They've ruined me, mate.'

# ❧CHAPTER SIX☙

**B**en made his way back to the station in a mood of despondency. His two favourite starting points, insurance fraud and the revenge of disgruntled employees, had both washed out, and he felt at a loss. Throughout his career in the police, he had always relied on the essential similarity of most crimes of a particular type; criminals, he had found, were seldom original thinkers. They were nearly always both lazy and stupid, which was, he thought, why they were crims instead of prospering at a normal job.

Uncomfortably aware of his new status as Computer Crime expert, he mounted the stairs to the C.I.B. office, hoping everyone else would be out. Lacking the faintest idea of how to trace the hack from the technical end, he was going to have to ring up one of the chaps he'd met on the course, admit his problem, and ask for help. There was, however, one faint hope remaining. Assuming that the person or persons responsible for the leak were genuine religious fanatics, they might possibly be found in the employ of the cloud company. At the very least, perhaps there had been other, similar incidents that might form a larger picture that would be helpful.

'B.U.M. Computing,' said a chirpy voice. 'How may I direct your call?'

'I want to talk to whoever's in charge of the Cloud Services,' said Ben firmly.

'Certainly, sir, I'll connect you to one of our salesmen.'

'No! No, this is about an existing account. This is Detective Constable Ben Jackson. Police business, so I'd like to speak to whoever's in charge of that area, please.'

'What's it regarding?'

'As I said, a police matter.'

There was a loud buzzing sound, and presently some very annoying elevator music came on the line, blasting out at four times the previous volume. Ben put down the receiver and went to make himself a coffee; he could still hear it perfectly well from the other side of the squad room.

Twenty-seven minutes later he was still on hold, listening to the elevator music which was on a loop. Ben had timed the loop. Its duration was three minutes and twenty seconds. He hung up and dialled again.

'B.U.M. Computing,' said a chirpy voice. 'How may I direct your call?'

'Yeah, g'day. Ben Jackson here again. I think something went wrong. I was wanting the chap in charge of the cloud computing services.'

'Certainly, sir, I'll connect you to one of our salesmen.'

This time, it went to the music before he could say anything. He waited ten minutes, then hung up and dialled again.

'B.U.M. Computing,' said a chirpy voice. 'How may I direct your call?'

'It's about the Yarralove account,' Ben ground out. 'Put me through to the manager.'

The elevator music reappeared. This time, it only cycled through its loop twice.

'B.U.M. Computing,' said a chirpy voice.

'How may I direct your call?'

Ben slammed down the phone. The beginnings of a headache pounded behind his eyes. He would have to go there in person. The card Max Panagiotidis had given him had an address in South Melbourne, a good five hours away by car. It would make more sense to get one of the local chaps to go. The trouble was, Ben was supposed to be nutting this out by being a computer expert. If he started putting in requests to other stations, the sergeant would know about it, and would, quite reasonably, want to know why he wasn't doing that. Although Ben knew he'd been sent on the course for a frivolous reason, the sergeant was now bragging all over the place about his foresight in getting a man qualified to handle this type of crime, and claiming he had predicted something like this was going to happen soon. It would be embarrassing for him if Ben revealed himself to be totally incompetent to do the job.

Getting on the sergeant's wrong side, Ben knew, would be a very bad move. The last time he had had the misfortune to do so, accidentally shooting himself in the leg and letting an armed robber escape, he'd wound up sitting in a vehicle every night with a bag of fish treats and a dog whistle. For six months. A fond smile crept onto his face as he remembered the days of Operation

Tomcat. The assignment had got him his little furry mate, and that, of course, had resulted in his meeting Tammy. It hadn't been all bad, but that didn't mean he was anxious to repeat the experience. If he got assigned to T.W.A.T. again, there was no telling when he'd get out. He probably never would. Visions of spending his entire working life staring at goats, or something equally stupid, flashed before his eyes.

There had to be another way. Ben glanced at the clock. It was a quarter to twelve. Had he really been sitting there for two hours? It would be lunchtime soon. Lunchtime... that was it! He'd start calling again at twelve. Sooner or later that receptionist would be going to lunch, and then someone more helpful might be on the switch. He'd call every fifteen minutes until he got someone else.

***

Up in Yarrangong Heights, Donald Blackman was enjoying himself no end. 'WHORE SLEEPS WITH DOZENS OF MEN,' he typed. 'Says she specialises in husbands.' He started uploading the woman's photograph. Chuckling to himself, he wrote several paragraphs of outraged morality that he'd copied from the Westboro website, altering the focus slightly so that it was about adultery rather than gay people. He didn't take much trouble with it. He didn't think his readership was all that critical. The thing was to keep the pot boiling. Shirley Mills had mentioned that she and her husband were going to couples' counselling. The last thing he wanted was a reconciliation. That would end his fat family law matter for good and all. This ought to put a spoke in their wheel. He added the names of Mills and several other local businessmen, all with prosperous businesses and families. He had no factual basis for doing so, but he had realised that that didn't matter. There had already been fire, so additional smoke was a good thing. After all, he wasn't making a statement in court that he'd have to back up with evidence; it was all anonymous, so he could be as outrageous as he liked. So he ruined a few extra lives – so what? If they weren't playing around through Yarralove, they were probably doing it somewhere else. He turned to the listing he'd printed out, scanning for his next target.

***

Tammy stared around her bedroom. The fresh paint did look lovely; she'd added a subtle accent to the monochrome colour scheme by doing all the trim in high gloss and the walls in satin. It didn't make her as happy as she'd thought, though. Against the bright, white room her mattress on the floor, with the cardboard box holding her alarm clock and a couple of paperbacks, looked sad and rubbishy, as if someone had moved out and left behind things no longer needed or wanted.

She dropped into the kitchen chair at her card table desk and buried her head in her hands. The idea that she had to break up with Ben had become more entrenched in her mind with every day that passed, until she had, without ever making a conscious decision, accepted it as a given. She had been unable to speak of it to him when he'd come home, and all through that weekend, as they'd cooked together, and eaten, and made love, and slept entwined, and woken to the first song of magpies to make love again, she had pushed it to the back of her mind. It had been an idyllic weekend, and she had not been able to bear to spoil it. And then he'd already left for work when she'd woken up this morning.

Tom twined about her ankles, crying in almost inaudible tones. Failing to elicit a response, he gave a little chirping trill, jumped up to the table, scattering papers, and thrust his nose into her ear. Tammy buried her nose in soft fur and gave way to howls of misery, remembering her loneliness when she'd first moved here, grieving for her dead marriage and not knowing a soul, and the miracle of Tom's appearance. Against all probability, he'd ended up living with her, and now she was going to lose him, too. Her only friend, she sobbed to herself, aware of the melodrama in the thought but unable to control herself. And now she was going to be alone in the world again, after all the happiness and the security of her little family. It wasn't fair.

***

By three o'clock, when his shift finished, Ben had called B.U.M. Computing fifteen times, with results varying between three and thirty-five minutes on hold. The elevator music continued to play its sinister little melody in his head even when he hung up, like a vicious afterimage. This just wasn't working. He was going to have to get someone to go there. Or go there himself, somehow.

Going himself was out of the question. Sergeant Stevenson had rostered him on day shift all week to facilitate his enquiry, assuming that he would be spending his time either on his own computer or the client's computer. He couldn't get to Melbourne in business hours.

He couldn't request local police to visit the place because the Sergeant would find out, and he'd be in trouble. Or wait – would he? Stevenson didn't know jack about computers himself. If he said such and such an enquiry was necessary, that would be taken at face value. It felt a bit sneaky, but hey, thought Ben. Whatever it takes, right? Sergeant Stevenson had himself stressed how important it was to get a quick result.

Looked at in this light, the problem wasn't so desperate. He'd just sign out and go himself. He'd travel on his own time to ease his conscience. If he left very early he could be in South Melbourne by, say, eleven, and that would give him most of the day at B.U.M. if needed.

Cheered by having a plan of action, he left for home.

***

He heard the sobs before he was even all the way up the front steps. Mouth dry, heart pounding, he dropped his keys twice, and was on the verge of kicking in the door like a television cop by the time he managed to fit key to lock. He found Tammy in the bedroom, flat out over her writing table, crying as if her heart was broken. He stood for a moment in the doorway, frozen in panic despite his training. He had never seen Tammy cry. Even when she'd dropped the hammer on her bare foot she'd only let out a few choice words.

'Tammy, Jesus, what's happened? Is it Tom?' No, Tom was there, he now saw, crouched on the table, looking unhappy with his shoulder blades sticking up and eyes slitted. He seemed okay. Tammy didn't reply, unless a long, drawn-out wail could be considered a reply. Horrible thoughts flashed through Ben's mind. Was she ill? Did she have cancer? Oh God, was he going to lose her?

He pulled her into his arms, carrying her over to their bed, settling awkwardly onto the mattress. They really had to get some proper furniture. He could easily pay for it, if Tammy would let up on her obsessive independence.

He sat, holding her as tightly as he could without hurting her, until the storm passed, and she sat up a little, sniffing. He couldn't reach his handkerchief without letting go, and he didn't want to let her go, not just yet, not until he knew she was calm. He handed her the end of the sheet. She blew her nose on it, then sat, looking straight ahead, clutching the balled up sheet.

Ben's thoughts raced in small, terrified circles. It had to be either something medical, or a death in the family. When he spoke, it was in hushed, careful tones.

'Did you get some bad news?'

# ∽CHAPTER SEVEN∾

Tammy was stuck. She sat rigid on the edge of the mattress, clutching the sheet. She'd blown her nose on the sheet. How could she have done that? Now she'd have to change them.

She didn't know what to say to Ben, now that the moment had all too clearly arrived. The storm of weeping had left her drained, her mind fuzzy, and all she really wanted was to go to sleep. But there was Ben, poor Ben, obviously terribly worried, and of course he was doing exactly the right thing, just like he always did. Holding her and not pestering, waiting until she should feel ready to talk. Not pushing. Her Ben, the perfect partner. Fresh tears threatened, but Tammy was cried out.

***

Ben was stuck, caught in the moment, with no idea how to proceed. He had managed to wriggle backwards on the mattress till he could lean his back against the wall, supporting Tammy against his chest. He was tense, wired with anxiety, desperate to know the cause of her distress. His suit was getting all crushed and wrinkled, but he didn't dare move. He'd have to hang it up in the bathroom and hope the shower would steam it out. He had only the one suit, because his other one, a light grey, had been ruined with indigo dye when he'd apprehended a shoplifter. He hadn't been able to afford to replace it just at first, and then he'd been sent off on the course, where he had survived by changing out of his one remaining suit each evening and sending it for pressing by the hotel's valet service, a convenience which was added to his bill and would be paid for by the Police Department, as long as Sergeant Stevenson did not scrutinise the bill too closely.

With an effort, he kept his breathing slow and even, straining to instil calm in Tammy. She was leaning heavily against him now, her breathing evening out, and she wasn't far off the sleep of exhaustion. He resigned himself to not finding out what was wrong until much later in the evening, perhaps even the next day if she slept right through. Over the next half hour, by tiny increments, he shifted out from under her until she was lying on the mattress. Carefully he got up; with infinite slow gentleness he undid her laces and eased off her shoes. Then he tiptoed from the room and pulled the door to. Let her sleep it off.

His planned trip to Melbourne was hopeless now. He couldn't leave Tammy alone in such distress. He felt like crying himself, from nerves and pent-up fear. Cancer, whispered the back part of his brain, the part from which nightmares slink out in the small hours of the morning.

He filled the kettle and switched it on, closing the kitchen door lest its whistling wake Tammy. He needed to think about the case, and he needed to think about other things, too.

An hour later, he had verified what he'd suspected; his private health insurance didn't cover her.

All through the long and silent afternoon and evening, despite his resolution to think about the case, Ben thought about Tammy. He worried at the problem like a small dog with a rubber bone, making no impression upon it. He had rung up the insurance company, but they had only verified what he'd known already; if Tammy was already ill, he couldn't add her to his policy. He'd taken inventory of his assets. There were not many. Although Ben had been in the police force for all of his working life, he was only twenty-eight, and his savings were – well, just what you'd expect from a cheerful soul who liked a good time and didn't worry much. He was a grasshopper, he thought with shame, not an ant. He had about thirty thousand in term deposits, a recent model Commodore, and his superannuation, which he could not touch. If Tammy needed expensive operations, he couldn't afford many of them. Ben had no idea what an operation cost. He thought it might be about ten thousand dollars.

He glanced at his watch. It was getting on for six. Better do something about dinner.

Using his hard-won culinary skill (there was only one of it) Ben constructed Spaghetti Bolognese. When he had finished, there was not a clean or empty surface in the entire kitchen. He laid the table and went to look in on Tammy.

She had curled into a ball and pulled the doona up over her head. Ben didn't know whether to wake her for dinner or let her sleep. He dithered in the doorway for a few minutes, and finally tiptoed away. He could heat up her meal when she did wake.

He went and sat at the kitchen table, among the results of his cooking. The kitchen was a mess, he realised. Tammy wouldn't like that. When she cooked, somehow there never seemed to be any mess. His mum was the same. It was some kind of skill that women had, some Secret Women's Business thing they did when you weren't looking. He'd have to do it the hard way.

As he washed up all the dishes, in no particular order, Ben made a determined effort to stop his mind from running around in circles. Resolutely he pushed away the image of a white and emaciated Tammy in a hospital bed, and the even worse image of a flower-strewn coffin. There were plenty of other things that might have upset her. Perhaps one of her parents had died. He remembered with a pang that they still hadn't met each other's parents. There had always seemed to be plenty of time. He hoped he wouldn't be meeting Tammy's mum for the first time at her dad's funeral.

***

Tammy felt disconnected and weird when she woke. It was full dark, the uncurtained windows solid squares of black in the dim light from the hall. She stood up, staggering a little, her legs weak, as if she had been ill for a long time.

She found Ben in the kitchen, hunched over the table, staring at nothing. There was a smell of cooking, and pots on the stove. He'd made spag bol. The spaghetti had not been drained, and was swollen to mush, completely inedible. Water dripped off the counters and there were sauce splatters all over the stove. The fluorescent light was very bright.

Seeing her, Ben jumped up, and his face blossomed into that beautiful smile. He lifted Tom off his lap and placed him gently on the floor, then crossed the tiny kitchen in a couple of strides to pull her into a careful hug. For a second his lips rested on her forehead, then he drew back to peer worriedly into her face.

'Are you feeling better?'

Tammy sighed, and shrugged. She wasn't feeling better, and didn't think she ever would be. She went to the stove and started to drain out the now-cold spaghetti.

'I made dinner.'

'Yeah, I see that. This spaghetti's had it, you have to drain it as soon as it's cooked. I'll make some more.' Horrified at how ungracious she was being, still she went on. 'Christ, what a mess. Water everywhere. What did you do, wash up with the garden hose?'

She watched the happiness drain out of Ben's face. It was a physical thing, like water running out of a bucket with a hole at the bottom. She felt like a murderer. She had done that, she had made the hole, leaked out his happiness. It was like kicking a puppy. She hated herself, but couldn't seem to stop. Where had their easy camaraderie gone? They had always been such friends. She ran fresh water into the pot and lit the gas under it. Ben obviously hadn't eaten yet, or the spaghetti would have been drained. He must have been waiting for her. God, it was after eight, he must be starving. She felt the tiny bit worse that was possible in her state.

'Tammy.' When he spoke, his voice was rusty, grating. 'Won't you tell me what's wrong? I hate seeing you like this. Please?'

She sat at the table opposite him. Hunched over her folded arms, staring at the floor, to Ben she looked the picture of misery.

'Are you... are you sick?'

A tiny shake of the head.

'Did you have bad news, then? Someone die, is that it?'

Another shake.

'Did something happen at work? Did you lose your job?'

She looked up for a moment, staring wild-eyed.

'You lost your job. Don't worry about that, come on Tammy, you know I'll look after you. Anyway, you'll easily get another one. Tell you what, one of the blokes at work, his brother's an accountant, I can ask him, maybe they need a secretary or something. It'll be fine, you'll see. And with you working days, we'll be able to do more stuff in the evenings. Go out more.'

The water had come to the boil, and he got up to turn down the gas. As he lowered spaghetti into the pot, pushing down the ends with a fork, he almost missed the low mutter.

'I didn't lose my job, it's not that.'

Ben span around, waving the fork. 'Well, what bloody is it then? I come home and find you in a bloody hysterical state, you won't tell me what the matter is, what the hell am I supposed to think?' Becoming aware of how ridiculous he looked, he tossed the fork into the sink. 'Just tell me, Tammy. I can handle it. Whatever it is. But this, I can't handle.'

Now she was crying again. Oh, great job, Ben, he thought. Congratulations, big man, you made your girlfriend cry.

He wrapped his arms around her and squeezed gently. 'Come on, Tammy, please, no more crying, okay? You're gonna make yourself sick. And you're upsetting Tom.' Having played this ultimate trump card, he looked about. Where was the little guy, anyway? Must have gone out. Must get a proper catflap instead of that broken pane, he chided himself. Do it this weekend. Maybe surprise her with it, that would be the thing, fix it while she's out at work.

She sniffed, wiped her nose on his shirt and sat up, pulling away from him.

'Okay. Now, can you tell me what's got you in such a state? You don't have to go into all the details, but just a hint? You're scaring me.'

'I can't, Ben, I just can't, not now. Please, I just can't.'

Ben sighed and went back to the stove. Sadly he turned on the gas under the sauce, gave it a quick stir and set about putting together a salad. As he worked, he talked, quietly, almost to himself.

'I don't mean to push you. I can see you're upset. See, that's what breaks me up, seeing you like this. I mean, every day I come home, you're always here, and you're always happy to see me, and that's the thing, see, it's happy. Our life. You and me. Right from the start. First time I saw you, I thought you looked like you were a happy person. I thought, I want to know this woman. And the way Tom took to you. He doesn't just like everyone, you know. He could be a real little shit sometimes. Last girlfriend I had, you didn't see him for dust if I brought her home. Then he'd wee on the carpet. One time he sprayed on her handbag. God, I was so embarrassed. She looked up and caught him doing it. That's why she broke up with me. Not right away, but she couldn't get the smell out. I offered to replace it, but it was some kind of special one. A herpes bag, I think she said.' Was that a tiny chuckle? Don't look round. Just keep talking. 'So, anyway. Me and you. It was just so perfect. Right from the start. You got on with all my mates, you were a fantastic cook, and the way you look... at first, I kept waiting for the wrong thing to crop up, like you'd be off with other guys, or you'd be nasty when you got drunk, or you'd be a bitch to other women or something, but just nothing, you really were that perfect. You really are that perfect, and I can't believe how lucky...' he realised he was crying himself, silent tears running down his face. 'Shit.' His nose was running, too. He wiped it on his sleeve. The sauce was boiling and the spaghetti looked done. He turned off the gas and reached for the colander, sneaking a look at Tammy as he turned. She sat motionless, her face unreadable. But at least she was looking at him.

# CHAPTER EIGHT

It wasn't until after a silent Tammy had left for work that it hit Ben. The idea struck him with the force of a tsunami, and he stood in the kitchen, a teabag in one hand, mouth open, marvelling at how he could have been so blind, so incredibly stupid.

It all made sense now – the tears, the sleeping, the not being able to talk about it.

Tammy was pregnant.

He was going to be a father.

As if sleepwalking, he stumbled into the sitting room and sat down on the sofa. He looked around him. Everything seemed new. How lucky, he thought, that they were so light on furniture. There would be plenty of room for a playpen; the kitchen was too small, but Tammy would be able to keep an eye on their child from there easily, through the serving hatch.

She must not be too far along, he reckoned. That was why she wouldn't tell him. In case... Ben shivered. His sister had lost her first, early on. She had sworn afterwards that when she got pregnant again she wouldn't tell Mike until she was three months. Ben had argued with her. He didn't think it would be fair to keep it from him. It was a husband's right to know, he had said. Even if it was bad news and would make him unhappy. Especially then. You got married for better or worse, he had said. His sister had scoffed at him, calling him an idealist. Men were not tough enough to take that kind of thing, she had said. Ben had been affronted. Hadn't he not even cried when he accidentally shot himself in the leg? He was plenty tough. Then she had scoffed even more. It went with being the older sister, he supposed. To her he was always going to be a chubby-cheeked little nuisance, trailing after the big kids. She had visited him in hospital and scolded him for 'playing with guns', completely ignoring the fact he'd been in hot pursuit of an armed robber.

***

Tammy's arms ached from stretching up to the top shelf with tins of coconut cream. Did anyone actually buy the stuff? They must do, she supposed, as the shelf needed refilling. She was no nearer to telling Ben than she had been. Life was so unfair, she thought. You get a cheating fucker like Neville, who makes your life a misery, and you think the sun shines out of his arse until you catch him boffing your friend on your own kitchen table. Then you find the perfect man and you can't even be in love with him.

'Yo, bitch!' said Andy, coming up behind her and seizing her in a bear hug. 'What be a-happening, homie?'

Tammy rolled her eyes and elbowed him to make him let go. Turning, she surveyed him. 'Honestly Andy, you are so bogus. What's this new look? Rastafarian wannabe?'

'Rastaman be cool, dude. So cool, like ice.' Andy had tortured his blond hair into messy-looking dreadlocks, and topped them with a fuzzy knitted hat in many colours. It was felted by careless washing, and when she looked closely, she could see a little slit on one side.

'Um, Andy, you do realise that's a tea cosy you're wearing, right?'

'A what? I got it at Vinnie's.' He pulled it off his head and examined it. 'No label, but it fits alright.'

'It's meant to go over a teapot. To keep the tea warm. It's not a hat.'

'Whatever. Hey, I didn't tell you my news!' He danced a little jig, evidently forgetting his Rastafarian pose. 'I've got a job!'

'Gees, what a surprise. Cause here we are, at work.'

'Nooooo! A real job. With a firm. Blackman Lawyers. As a paralegal!'

'Oh, Andy, that's wonderful! When do you start?'

'Monday. Monday morning. Isn't it cool? Right here in town.'

'That really is fantastic. But what about your course?'

'I can still do it. I might have to cut back to two subjects instead of three, I'll see how I go this semester. But the lectures are all on the weekends anyway, and I can get last year's off people who've recorded them. It'll be fine. Think of the experience!'

'Yeah, great. Congratulations! Um... Andy,

you're not going looking like that, are you?'

'Like what?' He looked down at himself. 'You think the Hawaiian shirt's too loud?'

'The shirt, the tracky pants, the sneakers... the dreads... the tea cosy... I mean, don't get me wrong, but I don't think it's quite the look a conservative law firm is going for. I can't even see how you got hired if you went to the interview looking like that.'

'Oh. Well, I didn't, see, that was last week when I still had the Preppy thing going on. You don't think they'll like it?'

'No, Andy, I really don't. You want to fit in with the other lawyers. Anyway, this Rastafarian thing just isn't working for you. It's too surfacey. You know what you want? Remember a couple of months ago when you saw Wall Street and you had that corporate look?' It was no use, Tammy knew, just telling him to get a haircut and put on a suit and tie. With Andy, it had to be a *look*. His look of the moment generally depended on what movie he'd seen on late-night television.

'I dunno, Tam. I went to a lot of trouble to make these dreads.'

Tammy had a brainwave.

'But Andy. It's culturally insensitive. Law

firms can't afford that. You don't know who you might offend.'

'What cultural? What insensitive?'

'Well, dressing up as other people's cultures is culturally insensitive. I read a big thing about it on the net. Some American celebrity was copping nine kinds of flak for dressing up in a Native American headdress. See, it offends the Native American people when their sacred items are used by other people for fancy dress. And Rastafarians... you do know it's a religion, right? It's not just dressing up and talking a certain way.'

Andy looked blank. What a child he was, she thought fondly. God knew what kind of a lawyer he would make. She pressed her advantage.

'You make a statement with the way you dress, you know that, right? Well, the statement you want to make at Blackman Lawyers is that you're smart, professional and reliable. But most of all, that you're one of them. That's what all that "dress for the job you want" thing is about. Fitting in. Being recognised as a member of the pack. What did the person who interviewed you have on?'

'Mr Blackman? Um, dark grey suit, white shirt, red tie.'

'You see?'

Andy sighed. 'It's so boring.'

'Cheer up. Think of the money you'll be making. So when are you leaving?'

'Leaving? Here, you mean? I'm not, well not entirely, I'm just cutting back to three shifts a week, all night shift. See, then if it doesn't work out, I can come back full time, go back on days and everything's still in place, superannuation, leave, all that. Anyway – I better get on. See you at break.' He sauntered off down the aisle, in a weird, waddling gait that Tammy supposed was meant to look tough. Bless him. She felt very old and wise as she watched him go.

At break time, when everyone piled out the back door to smoke, Tammy checked her phone. There were three missed calls from Ben. The first message said he loved her, and hoped she wasn't overdoing things at the supermarket. The second message, time-stamped three minutes later, reminded her not to lift anything heavy. The third message, which had been left at five minutes to midnight, told her that whatever happened, she was always his Number One, and that she should by no means lift anything heavy. Tammy groaned. What was all this about heavy boxes? They did have a union, after all. The boxes of stuff were all on big trolleys that they pulled around, and those were loaded by a large, brawny man who taught Karate when he was not working here, and tossed the heaviest boxes about with gay abandon, as if they were boxes of tissues. He didn't come out for smoke breaks, because he used those as an opportunity to knock off a couple of hundred pushups. Once, when Tammy had had a flat tyre and couldn't find her jack, he had picked up the front end of her car and stood patiently holding it while a couple of the other blokes changed the wheel. She wondered what Ben was on about, and this in turn reminded her of how miserable she was about breaking up with him, and caused tears to start, which she had to pass off as smoke in her eyes.

It was too late to call back, she thought with relief. And he'd be fast asleep when she got home, and if she went straight to bed, she'd already be asleep when he got up for work in the morning, so she had until tomorrow night to figure out what to say. Again she ran over her reasoning in her mind, poking at it as if it were a sore tooth. Again she could find no flaw in it. It just couldn't be real love. Every romance novel she'd ever read, every movie she'd ever seen, had drama, tension, insuperable obstacles that were only overcome in the final scene. Not the quiet build of quotidian happiness with never a ripple, as she had had with Ben. Not that recognition, that instinctive familiarity, as if coming home from a long and harrowing journey to a place much loved. If only she could just stay with him, follow that quietness, that inner sense of right, and see where it led. But it wasn't fair to Ben, she knew. One day, True Love would happen, and then she'd have been just using him as a place marker. You couldn't do that to a person, especially not one you – no, she told herself firmly. She didn't love him, not really, she couldn't, or there would be all the tears and drama.

Break time was up. Tammy shuffled after the others, back to the endless lanes of shelves.

***

The week passed somehow. Every day, Tammy braced herself to sit down with Ben when he got home from work, and every day she chickened out. There was always something that stopped her. Ben had brought her home a bottle of special vitamin pills. Ben had volunteered to clean the bathroom, although it was her turn. Ben had brought her flowers. Every day when he got home, he insisted on giving her a foot massage. You would think she was sick, the way he fussed, constantly checking whether the temperature was right for her, jumping up to open windows or fetch a lap rug. He bought her an expensive pair of sheepskin moccasins that were heaven on her feet. He ran out to the shops whenever she fancied anything they didn't have, and he had even taken to putting the toilet seat down. He had always been a sweet and considerate soul, but now he was off the radar, in Mother Hen territory.

***

Blackman had a good week. He had hired a law student to do some of the scut work, so there were now two menials for him to bully. The new kid was irritating and seemed to have a screw loose, but he was, Blackman had to admit, good-natured, punctual and a quick study. By Friday, he had settled in so well that Blackman could hardly remember him not being there, and the office had taken on a calmer atmosphere. There was something about this that Blackman found deeply annoying. The kid was useful enough for a second-year student, although his citing of obscure caselaw that had nothing to do with anything at every opportunity made Blackman want to scream. His actual work, however, was fast and faultless, and Blackman had been reduced to grumbling about the smell of his aftershave. He left early, after threatening both Andy and Shelley with the sack if the smell of it wasn't gone by Monday.

***

The week passed somehow. Every day, Ben braced himself for Sergeant Stevenson's enquiry. 'How's it going with the hacker, Ben?' he would say, at varying times of the day. He made a point of not asking more than once a day, but Ben had an oppressive sense of him always lurking behind his closed office door, and took to circumnavigating the squad room to get to his desk, to avoid passing too close to Stevenson's door.

As far as the investigation was concerned, he had fallen into a routine. First check the day's paper and the godhateswhores website for anything new. Then, call B.U.M. On the third day, he had finally got through to someone. The B.U.M. technical people were now attempting to trace the hack, but so far they had had no success. Then, Ben would resume his usual police routine. He was working his way through the people affected, trying to come up with a list of suspects. So far he had drawn a blank; both the mayor and Mills had plenty of business rivals, but as they were not in the same business there was no overlap, and the school teacher didn't have any business rivals at all, and had only moved to Yarrangong at the beginning of the year.

By Friday, he had even interviewed Mills' and Polk's wives, with no result other than a harrowing experience with Mrs Polk's three West Highland Terriers, who had taken exception to him. The investigation was stalled, and he had no idea what to do.

# CHAPTER NINE

Tammy was at work on her book when he came home, clutching an enormous bunch of the fanciest flowers they had at the supermarket. He couldn't afford the florist; he was being as economical as he could, ready for the expenses that a new baby would incur. They'd have to do up a room for it, buy furniture, at least a cot, and there'd be medical expenses, and he didn't know what else. He wanted to ask his sister, but didn't dare; saying anything to anyone when Tammy hadn't told him seemed like bad luck, and he was having enough bad luck already at work without adding to it in any way.

Over dinner, he confided to her his worries about the case. 'I just can't see any way forward,' he moaned. 'Everything I think of just goes to a dead end. The Bum people reckon whoever hacked in there must be a real expert.'

Tammy was interested, despite her depression, which had not lifted, although most of the time she managed to shove it to the back of her mind. It was alien to her nature to be down for long, and day by day her natural cheerfulness reasserted itself, so that by the end of the week she seemed to Ben to be almost back to her normal self. It nagged at her during the nights, though, at work, and in the early mornings, when she was trying to sleep. In an effort to distract herself she had changed her usual headphone fare when at work, replacing the works of Anthony Trollope with a playlist of bright, cheerful music, most of which she had downloaded illegally from the internet.

'What about the organisation? This wacko church or whatever it is?'

'It doesn't exist, Tammy. I rang up the Australian Council of Churches, they've never heard of it. And this Reverend Phillips bloke who's supposed to be the head of it, I can't find anything about him anywhere. Either it's an alias, or he doesn't exist either.'

'They went to a lot of trouble for this, whoever they are. Someone has to have got something out of it.'

'Yeah, but what? None of these people seem to have any real enemies.'

'What about profit? Or maybe they're just genuine wackos and they're like, on a mission for God to clean up Australia.'

'I dunno. It just doesn't feel right. It's too... too targeted, you know?'

'No, I don't know. Didn't you say the website was full of all kinds of right wing stuff? Stop the boats, hate the Muslims and so on?'

'Well yeah, but not particular boats. Not particular Muslims. Now all of a sudden they're going after these guys in a small town in country Victoria. It's a change of texture, does that make sense? It sticks out.'

'Well, sure it does, it sticks out because they've committed a crime hacking into that website.'

Ben screwed up his face in frustration. His policeman's nose told him the dating agency hack was a different kind of thing than the racist and morality articles in the rest of the website, but he couldn't, somehow, explain this. It was a matter of a sort of difference in texture. Like running your hand along a rack of cotton shirts and suddenly coming to a woollen sweater. It felt like that in his mind, that sudden difference.

'I can't explain, Tammy. It's a cop thing. You get a sort of instinct. I dunno.'

'Yeah, right. You've been watching too many movies, Detective Boy.'

***

They spent the weekend in a nervous half-silence, each afraid to disturb the fragile status quo. Ben cleaned out the gutters, mowed the lawn (waiting until Tammy was awake, but not working on her book, lest the noise disturb her) and washed the outsides of all the windows. Tammy ironed Ben's shirts with especial care, and sewed on several buttons. They had never really discussed the division of household labour, but had fallen naturally into the separation of jobs into 'man stuff' and 'woman stuff' that both sets of their parents had used.

There was one important omission, though, in the habits of labour division Ben and Tammy had inherited from their respective parents. Neither household had kept any animals. And so it was that, preoccupied as each was with being the Ideal Partner and not treading on any toes, it was not until Saturday evening that it became apparent that Tom was not in the house.

They had planned to spend the evening at the Commercial Club, where a Latin dance night was to be held. Tammy was putting the final touches to her makeup when Ben, freshly showered and shaved and smelling of sharp lemon cologne, came into the bathroom, frowning.

'Have you seen Tom?'

'Tom? Isn't he on his chair?'

'No, he isn't, and he was still out when I went to bed last night. I left his dinner out for him.'

'That's funny. It was there when I got home, and it looked a bit manky so I chucked it out. I thought it must have been a second helping.'

'No, that was his dinner. It's not like him, now I come to think of it he wasn't there when I got home. Usually he comes running out to say hello.'

Tammy drew in a careful breath. She wanted to scream. Why had he waited until now to mention it? And why had she, so wrapped up in her private misery, failed to notice that Tom wasn't there? She was a terrible mother. Panic beat in her veins, and her hands clenched on the edge of the basin. All kinds of dreadful scenarios flashed across her mind, each more horrible than the last. Tom had been killed on the road. He was injured and dying and hiding in a hole somewhere, crying and wondering why they didn't come for him. He had been lured into the clutches of some evil maniac who would use him for laboratory experiments.

Through a dark mist, she became aware of strong hands supporting her. She was sitting on the edge of the bath, bent over. A warm hand on the back of her neck urged her head down.

'That's right. Take deep breaths. In and out, that's the way.'

Dimly, Tammy wondered how one might be expected to breathe, if not in and out. Sideways? Round in a circle? That was how you played the didgeridoo, wasn't it, circular breathing? She felt the sensation of the hard, cold bathtub rim drift away.

***

She woke quite suddenly, alarmed and disoriented to find herself lying on their mattress. Her dress was rucked up under her thighs, the material wadded uncomfortably. Damn it, fresh from the cleaners and now it would be unwearable. Her shoes were off, she noticed.

Then memory slammed down, and she drew in a gasping breath.

'Steady there, don't start hyperventilating.' Ben was sitting on the floor by her head. 'Can you sit up? Here, I'll help you.'

Wondering, Tammy allowed herself to be assisted upright, and accepted the glass he offered her.

'Go on, drink it, it's just water. You fainted.'

'Tom... we have to look for him. He might be hurt, anything...'

'Yeah, I know, I'm worried too but there's no use making yourself sick, specially now, in your condition.'

'Condition? What condition?'

Ben flushed scarlet. It was a thing he never could control. She remembered with faint amusement their first meeting, when he'd revealed the embarassing details of his job at the time. Beetroots hadn't been in it.

'Well, never mind that. The thing is, you're worrying too much. We'll easily find him. I already called Macka.'

'Macka? What's he got to do with it?' Macka had been his partner, she recalled, in the days of Operation Tomcat, when they'd sent Tom out with his high-tech digicam collar to collect data on criminals. The operation hadn't been a success, hence Tom's early retirement.

'Cause he's got the car, see? The one with the special tracker installed.'

Tammy shook her head, baffled.

'Tammy, don't you see? He's still wearing the collar.'

He was right, she realised with a flood of relief. He was still wearing it, the pretty diamante collar that camouflaged a wealth of miniaturised technology. Including a GPS location thingy. Also including, she remembered with horror, a video recorder. One that transmitted on a narrow band and was received by the special equipment in the T.W.A.T. mobile station. How, she wondered, could she have forgotten about that? She had just been so used to seeing him in it, and it didn't bother him, so she'd never taken it off.

'Macka said he'll be over in half an hour. We'll find him, don't worry. He's probably got himself locked into someone's garden shed or something.'

***

Macka arrived well inside the stated time, in an unmarked car. Ben and Tammy piled in. There had been some argument about Tammy's presence on the mission, but she had refused to stay quietly at home as Ben had urged. Now, her going-out makeup and styled hair a strange contrast to her old tracksuit, she sat and jittered on the back seat.

They drove in widening circles for forty-five minutes before Ben picked up a faint signal on the tracker.

'Hang on, I'm getting something... keep going straight for a bit... yep, hang a left, he's over that way.'

'Over on nob hill, looks like,' said Macka. 'Maybe your accommodations weren't posh enough for him. Hey, see if you can pick up on the camera feed.'

Ben fiddled with knobs. 'Yeah, I've got signal... can't make anything out, though. Must be dark where he is.'

A horrible realisation came to Tammy. 'Oh my God, Ben. He's still wearing the camera.' She punched him, hard, in the shoulder.

'Ow! What was that for? Don't jog me, I've got to concentrate on this.'

'He's still wearing the camera, Ben. The camera. You bastard.'

'What? What's the matter?'

'You know what's the matter, Ben. The bloody camera. He's been in the bedroom when we – oh, God. I suppose I've got bloody sex tapes all over the net.' She punched him again, harder.

'Right, hang a left, Macka.'

'Don't worry, Tammy,' said Macka, swinging the big car around. 'That equipment's just been gathering dust out the back. No one's been using it since Operation Tomcat finished.'

'Go right. Slow down, it's really strong now.'

Tammy subsided, muttering, thinking about Tom's habit of sitting on the side of the tub while she had her bath. Bloody cops with their silly bloody operations. She prayed Macka was telling the truth about the equipment. What if there were sex tapes, and her parents saw them? Or Neville? She couldn't bear it.

'Okay, back up a bit. Or, look, go down the end and chuck a u-ey.'

Of course, Tammy thought, if it hadn't been for Operation Tomcat, she'd never have met Tom at all. Or Ben, she reminded herself. Anyway, it was Tom who was important now, and as soon as they got him back, she promised herself, she'd do something about that bloody camera.

'Right, I reckon this is the place.'

Macka craned sideways to look at the box. 'Yeah, I reckon. Right, what's the plan now?'

'Just go and ring the doorbell, I reckon.'

They piled out of the car and stood in the street.

'There's no lights on,' Tammy pointed out. 'Just the front porch light. It's still early, they must be out.'

'Nine-oh-seven,' said Macka. 'Saturday night. Fair bet.'

'Well, might as well give it a go,' said Ben. They trooped up the path. There were two doors to the outside, one opening from a single-storey part of the big house that jutted out from one side. The front entrance was a huge, arched double door, its Tudorish construction contrasting oddly with the Spanish-inspired rendered building. A massive lantern hung from the porch roof, and two bracketed lamps of similar style illuminated each side of the second door.

They clustered in the porch. Ben pressed the doorbell. From somewhere inside, a few bars of the 1812 Overture could be dimly heard. Macka snorted. 'Bloody pretentious shit. I bet that gets old real quick, hearing that all the time.'

'Shh, quiet,' said Tammy. 'They'll hear you.'

They waited. Nothing happened. 'Try it again,' said Tammy. Macka pressed the button again, holding it down so the music repeated again and again.

'Steady on,' said Ben. 'No sense annoying them.'

But there was no response.

'They must not be home,' said Ben.

'Well, derr,' said Tammy. 'It's easy to see you're a detective.'

'Don't be like that. Let's try the other door.'

'What for? They're obviously not home.'

'Check all the options,' said Ben. 'It's procedure. Besides, this part looks separate, it might be a flat with someone else living in it.'

'What, like a granny flat?' said Macka. 'They're usually out the back.'

He pressed the doorbell on the other door, which wasn't all that much smaller. It was then that

Tammy noticed the brass plate.

'What's this?' she said, peering at it. 'Hey, it's an office. Blackman Lawyers.'

She was unprepared for the reaction of Ben and Macka.

'Holy shit,' said Macka, jumping back as if stung. Ben moaned faintly.

'What's the matter?' she asked. 'It's just some lawyer. Shut now, anyway.'

'You don't know this guy,' said Macka, shuddering. 'He's an evil bastard.'

Ben shook his head. 'Remember that time he had Jules on the stand? Made her cry. She was in floods, in front of everyone in the County Court. He's vicious.'

'So what? We're not doing anything wrong.' Tammy pressed her ear to the door. 'Hang on, shut up a minute, will you?' Was that a faint wail? 'Tom, is that you, sweetie? Tom-Tom. Puss puss puss puss puss...'

'Jesus, Tammy, don't make so much noise. We don't want to attract attention.'

'Quiet!' hissed Tammy, gesturing frantically.

From inside the building came a faint, wailing cry.

# ℬCHAPTER TEN℘

Everyone retreated to the car to discuss the situation. Tammy was in favour of breaking in through the window she'd noticed on the front wall of the office. This was immediately vetoed by Ben and Macka, on the grounds of being police officers. Tammy argued necessity, and Defence of Another; Macka countered with the 100% probability of them both getting the sack.

Macka, who had no personal stake in the matter beyond not getting caught unauthorisedly borrowing the T.W.A.T. tracking equipment, was in favour of leaving the whole matter. Blackman was bound to discover the cat on Monday morning, he said, and would either eject it forthwith or ring up the pound. All they had to do was wait until they got a call, since Tom was microchipped.

Against this was Ben's greater familiarity with Blackman. He wouldn't put it past Blackman, he said, to Do Something Awful. Blackman was a Nasty Bit of Work. Tammy burst into tears and implored them to Do Something, Right Now. The interior of the car took on a steamy feeling.

Eventually, after more tears from Tammy and a declaration from Macka that he would have nothing more to do with the matter, they reached a compromise. Ben would go and call on Blackman at his residence the following day, and would claim that they had driven around town searching for Tom and had heard him cry from within the office. Blackman would then open the office and all would be well. Tammy said it would be better if she went, as Blackman did not know her at all, and might be more sympathetic to a woman. Ben vetoed this on the grounds that she couldn't even begin to imagine how nasty Blackman was and he didn't want her upset in her condition. Then he went bright red again.

What was this condition he kept banging on about, Tammy wondered. And why was Macka carrying on and congratulating him? And congratulating her? They were both insane, she decided. It must be the stress. Never mind that.

'Look, can't you two idiots keep your minds on

the job? Wait, Macka, what are you doing?' Macka had started the engine and was pulling away from the kerb. 'Hang on, go back, I need to speak to Tom, tell him we'll get him in the – dammit, go back!'

'Settle down, Tammy, he'll be okay for one night. We can't have some old biddy from Neighbourhood Watch calling the police because we're creeping around an empty house. Besides, Macka needs to get the control box back before it's missed.'

She threw herself back against the seat, huffing.

***

The rest of the evening passed in a miserable fog. It was too late to go out dancing as they'd planned, and neither of them felt like it anyway, or like anything else. They made an effort, putting on a movie and ordering pizza, but Tammy felt Ben wasn't really concentrating on the film any more than she was. Tom usually sat on the back of the sofa when they watched television, and she missed the tickling of his tail swishing on the back of her neck. They went to bed early, in silence, and Tammy lay on her back in the dark, listening to Ben's breathing and to the absence of purring, and trying not to think about Tom alone in the dark.

It was just as well, she thought, that she hadn't got up the courage to break up with him. They needed each other now. But then, when hadn't they? She had never felt so right, so happy and so comfortable, with anyone. More than anything, she wanted that rightness to be permanent. But then, true love. Mustn't forget that. You owed your partner honesty. She turned her pillow over again, flopping onto her stomach and letting out a huge sigh.

'Can't you sleep, either?' said Ben.

'Not really.'

'How about some Milo?'

In the dark, Tammy smiled. She had been on the point of suggesting just that.

In the kitchen, she heated milk while Ben got out the mugs and the big green can, working together with the smoothness of habit. They sat at the table, sipping Milo in comfortable silence. Outside, a magpie burst into joyful carolling. It couldn't be far off dawn.

This, Tammy thought. Just this. Priceless. If only Tom were here, it would be perfect.

For the first time, it occurred to her that perhaps her thinking hadn't been sensible. Suppose, she asked herself, just suppose I said screw true love, and just kept him? But then, honesty. It just wasn't fair to go on, letting him think she loved him when she obviously didn't. It was no way to treat someone you– well, not loved, of course, but someone you–

'Penny for them?' said Ben, crashing into her train of thought. Well, she'd think about it later.

'Oh, just – you know, Tom, and wondering whether he's hungry, and frightened...' The first lie, she accused herself. You just lied to Ben. You never did before. You horrible bitch. But what was the alternative? You could hardly break up with a man at a time like this; it would be too cruel for anything. Besides, she argued, she had been thinking about that, in the back of her mind. Sort of.

'Nah. He's asleep, I reckon. Like we would be if we had any sense.'

'Yeah, but we don't, do we?'

'Nup! No sense here!'

Wordlessly, Tammy reached for his hand. His warm, strong, familiar hand. And she sat there, clutching it, as outside, the sky coloured itself pink, and tree by tree, morning birds launched the day.

***

Ben drew in a deep breath, and let it out again. Then he repeated the process a few more times. In through the nose, out through the mouth. It was a remedy against fear that his grandmother had taught him, and though he'd seldom had occasion to use it, it had sometimes come in handy when sitting exams.

Not that he was afraid of Donald Blackman, he told himself sternly. Who was Blackman, anyway? Just a dodgy lawyer that no one liked. That no one likes because he's the devil incarnate, said a small voice at the back of his mind. That no one likes because he's a fat, mean prick, Ben corrected it. Determinedly conscious of his own slender non-meanness, he got out of the car and slammed the door. Best get it over with. After all, Blackman couldn't shoot him.

He marched up the path and rang the doorbell, listening as the tacky music died away and sneaking a glance at his watch. It was four and a half minutes before the door finally opened, revealing a bleary-eyed, unshaven mountain of a man, who smelled strongly of used alcohol. Funny how drink always smelt so different when it came out through the pores.

'Oh, hi, sorry to bother you. My name's Ben–'

'Not interested,' barked Blackman, starting to

close the door. Ben moved forward, not quite stepping into the doorway, which would be trespass, but triggering the unconscious half-step back from Blackman which prevented him from closing the door.

'It's our cat,' he said firmly. 'He's got himself shut up in your office at the front there. We've been looking for him for ages and we heard him crying in there last night. We rang, but you weren't home.' He saw Blackman's eyes narrow and talked on, meeting the objection he knew was coming. 'He's got a very loud voice, a real little shrieker he is. Probably because we never got him fixed. We'd best get him out of there before he sprays on anything.'

Blackman was now, he saw, envisaging the possible state of his office, and had forgotten about his suspicion, at least for the moment.

'Alright, just a minute while I get the keys. Christ, it's bloody early enough. You could have waited till a civilised time. Ten o'clock on a Sunday morning...'

'I was thinking of your carpets,' Ben called after him, grinning to himself.

Blackman returned with a bunch of keys, shouldering Ben rudely aside. 'He'd better bloody well not have sprayed, or you'll be in more bloody trouble...'

They entered the outer office. It looked and smelt normal enough, Ben saw with relief. Secretary's desk on one side, row of filing cabinets under the window, a small group of chairs around a coffee table near the door. God, Tammy had better have been right. Then he saw, through the door to the inner office, the overturned wastepaper basket. He took a few steps into the room. 'Tom?' he called softly. 'Come on to Daddy. Tom-tom, puss puss puss?'

A rustling sound could be heard from the inner office. Ben crossed the room in a few quick strides and stuck his head through the door. Tom was indeed there, racing around the room batting a screwed-up piece of paper. Ben seized him as he ran past, palming the paper and shoving it in his pocket. He didn't need Blackman screaming about a mess. Other balled-up papers were spilling from the wastebasket, but Tom had evidently selected this one. He held Tom against his chest and turned to Blackman.

'Here he is, little mongrel. Thank you so much.'

'Hang on – that's that bloody animal with the fancy collar! That fucking thing's been spraying on the door for – '

Ben pretended not to hear, shouting over the top of Blackman as he rushed for his car. 'Thanks again, better get him in the car before he bolts, thanks, bye!'

He escaped to his car while Blackman was still yelling about his door, and irresponsible keeping of animals, not even bothering with the carrier basket but tossing Tom into the back seat and taking off without his seat belt. He'd managed it without even saying his last name. With any luck Blackman would have no reason to connect him with the police. Even if he did, what could he say? He'd lost his cat and come to fetch him, and they'd searched about and Tammy had heard him crying. But it would be better, he knew, not to have to trot out this story under the critical eye of Sergeant Stevenson, or that of the even more formidable Senior Sergeant Donoghue.

***

Tammy had allowed herself to be persuaded to lie down and close her eyes while Ben showered and got ready. As soon as her head hit the pillow, a wave of fatigue had broken over her head, and she had dropped into a deep and dreamless sleep, waking only at the sound of Ben's car door slamming out the front. She bolted upright, startled and disoriented, with no sense of any time having passed since she had lain down. The day was well advanced, she saw, the light strong. She groped for her watch on the bedside box. Nine fifty-one. Damn, damn, damn. She had been determined to go with Ben, and he'd sneaked off without her.

Keep occupied, that was the thing, she told herself. Concentrate on every tiny action, look straight ahead. Get in the shower. Get dressed. Comb your hair. Make the bed. Put on the kettle. Kitchen floor could do with a scrub. Don't start crying again. Get the bucket, that's right. Stick in some Domestos. Start at the back corner.

She had scrubbed the tiny kitchen floor within an inch of its life, and was hunched over the table when she heard the car pull up, inhaling strong tea and staring at her watch, a litany of please, please, please, running in her head, formless prayer to a deity she'd pretty well ignored since high school. She wrenched open the door as Ben reached the bottom step, Tom draped over his shoulder like a fur stole. Thank God thank God thank God ran the litany. She met them halfway on the stairs, grabbing man and cat in a fierce hug. Mine. Safe. Oh, thank God.

# ುಂCHAPTER ELEVEN ಲ

Tammy swam up through layers of warm fuzziness. Tom was curled tightly against her shoulder, emitting little chirps, paws twitching as he hunted a dream mouse. She was well rested, warm, and so comfortable she couldn't even feel her body. She nuzzled into the black fur, smiling. All was right with her world. There was no need to get up just yet. She could stay here and enjoy this precious moment.

Tammy drifted, and as she drifted, it came to her just how tense she had become in the last weeks. Ever since she'd come to the terrible decision that she must break up with Ben because it wasn't True Love, she'd become more and more stressed and unhappy. Now, in the bliss of total comfort, she allowed herself to take a second look at that decision.

True Love, she thought. The highs and lows, the ups and downs, the emotional roller-coaster. All of the novel-worthy, film-worthy torment. Was it really all that wonderful? She had thought she'd found True Love with Neville, and her life had become a series of dreams given up, of little accommodations, of constantly tiptoeing around Neville's temper and his finicky demands. Under its influence she had allowed herself to be herded, little by little, into the Stepford existence of a Military Wife. She had lost touch with all her friends, and little by little, she had given up serious reading, falling into a steady diet of the whodunnits and bodice-rippers that made up the chief stock of the base bookshops. What had there been left of the Tammy who had marched in protests and sat up all night debating the nature of consciousness in grimy little cafés? When, exactly, had she given up on the idea of her Masters'? She might have found True Love, but it hadn't come free, or even cheap. It had come at the cost of almost everything that had defined her life Before Neville, and after that price had been exacted, little drop by little drop so that she hardly noticed it, True Love had vanished, and she'd ended up living on a shoestring, in a strange town, without a friend in the world.

And then, along had come Ben. Handsome, kind, laughing, easy-going Ben. Always in a good mood, always cheerful, thoughtful too, and what he had seen in her Heaven only knew, but the fact that he had seen whatever it was, that he continued to see it, was unarguable. With Ben, every day was sunny. There were never any tears, never any needling, no nasty little traps laid so that whatever she did she ended up feeling bad about herself. With Ben, she had slotted into a rich network of friends and colleagues, a ready-made social life where everyone seemed to like Ben and to be ready to like her too. If something went wrong, as it had done this weekend, he didn't get hysterical, didn't go pointing the finger of blame. He looked after her and he worked on solving the problem. And all without a cross word.

He could handle being laughed at, too. It was a good sign in a person, Tammy felt. She'd howled and howled when she'd first heard about Ben's then job, the appallingly tosserish Tactical Watch Alternative Taskforce. 'Oh my God,' she had shrieked. 'You're the Man from TWAT!' And all Ben had done was turn a shade brighter scarlet. If she had dared even the faintest snigger at Neville at his most pompous, she'd have been paying for it for weeks.

She looked at her life with Ben, and her life with Neville. What was the value of True Love, anyway? Wasn't it really just like the Chanel logo?

The knockoff bags, as far as she could see, were just as nice as the real thing, and without the steep price tag. She had always derided what she saw as the commercially-induced ridiculous label worship of sheeple. Had she fallen into the trap herself? Had she put up with all that shit from Neville just for a designer label?

Tammy tossed restlessly. A sudden, powerful longing for tea invaded her. She tried to drift back down into her comfortable doze, but the teapot was calling to her, its shrill voice insistent. She'd get up, make a nice strong pot of tea and think about this. She groped about for her watch on the cardboard box of books that was their bedside table. Her hand knocked something small to the floor, something that rustled faintly.

Intrigued, Tammy sat up and reached over the edge of the mattress. It was a ball of crumpled-up paper. Ben must have left it there when he'd emptied his pockets. It was a rigid habit, one of his few; every night when he went to bed, he would empty his trouser pockets, making a neat little cache on the corner of the box. Then he would carefully hang up his trousers, no matter how late it was or how strong the incentive to cast them recklessly aside. It was a habit, he had explained, born of having only one decent suit. In the morning, he reversed the process, loading up from his little stash of loose coins, wallet and phone. There was usually nothing else. Curious, she unfolded the crumpled ball.

***

Ben was not having a good day. He stood in front of Senior Sergeant Donoghue's desk, hands behind his back, feet shoulder width apart, in parade rest as he had done at the Police Academy when being berated by the P.E. instructor.

The fierce Donoghue, O.C. of the Yarrangong Police, was effectively now Ben's immediate superior, since the mild-mannered Stevenson had gone on leave on Friday, heading north to visit his married daughter and three grandchildren and get in some fishing. Ben bet Donoghue didn't have anything as normal as grandchildren. He did not like Donoghue, whose outbursts of temper were feared by the whole station. Ben's dislike had a more personal ground, though. It had been Donoghue who had initiated his transfer to the experimental technology division, T.W.A.T., condemning him to months of ridiculous and pointless shifts where he sat in an unmarked car listening to the audio pickup from a cat's collar. He did not like to remember those days; although it was his job in T.W.A.T. that had brought him Tom, and had resulted in his meeting Tammy, it had been a long, tough six months, with all his mates sniggering.

'...nothing, not a bloody thing! What the hell have you been doing all bloody day? Well? Well?'

Caught on the hop, Ben stammered something about interviewing suspects. It was not well received.

'Suspects! Suspects?' Donoghue's voice rose to a screech, cracking slightly. His face turned an alarming shade of purple, and little flecks of saliva sprayed out. 'If you have one sensible suspect, I'd very much like to hear about it. For God's sake, man, this is turning nasty! I've got the frigging mayor on the phone every second day.'

Ben muttered something about the early days of the investigation, which was not well received. Donoghue flung the telephone at his head. It fell short, stopped by the cord. Ben ducked hastily out of Donoghue's office. If challenged, he would say that the incoherent screams of rage had sounded to him like 'Get out of here and don't come back until I send for you.'

Rather than return to his desk and stare mindlessly at his computer screen, waiting for inspiration while Donoghue's eyes bored into his spine through the glass wall of his office, Ben decided to whiz home and take Tammy out to lunch. They'd both had a rough time, and she deserved a treat. It was eleven-thirty now; that would give her time to get changed and do all the girly primping by which she set such store. Ben couldn't tell the difference, himself. She looked just as good to him when she'd just woken up, with her hair in a sexy tangle, as when she was all ready for a night on the town. He knew better than to say so, however, and had learned to recognise the smell of hairspray as his cue to comment favourably on her appearance.

He'd take her to the Commercial Club, he decided. Not the bistro, but the posh, expensive Terrace. It looked out over the golf links, and the day was right – not too hot, not windy, a beautiful day to sit out and enjoy the sun and fresh air. Just a couple of hours of luxury. He wanted to see that careworn look drain away from Tammy's face. He wanted to see her brilliant smile again, and hear that big, loud laugh.

The house was quiet when he let himself in. He hoped she wasn't still asleep; he was already pushing things a bit going out for a long lunch when he was supposed to be working, and if it would take her an hour to get ready he'd be well into the red zone. But as he neared their bedroom door he could hear an irregular thumping, interspersed with the heavy breathing of effort. She must be cleaning –

well, a posh fancy lunch would be both a welcome break and a reward.

He was completely unprepared for what he found. Tammy was on her knees in the middle of the room, shoving clothes into an empty cardboard box. She must be having a clean-out, he thought fondly. How did I get so lucky, she keeps everything so nice all the time.

Then he realised they were his clothes. What the – oh, yeah, she must be going to paint the inside of the wardrobe. That was so like her, he thought fondly. Nothing by halves. But his gear was going to be in a hell of a state, the way she was shoving it in. He went to kneel beside her and reached to take his shirts back out of the box. 'Steady on there, you're crushing everything.'

Tammy gave a great leap at the sound of his voice, and sprang up to crouch in front of him. 'Like I care! Serves you right, you cheating fucker!' She had been crying, he now saw.

'What – Tammy, what on earth – what's wrong with you?' These were not the right words, he realised even as they left his mouth.

'You BASTARD! You lying, cheating FUCKER!' She punctuated each shriek with a garment flung at his head. *Everyone's throwing stuff at me today. What's that about?*

'Settle down, you're scaring Tom.' Tom was indeed crouched in the far corner of the mattress, his shoulder-blades an angular protest. Too late, he remembered how inflammatory it was to say 'settle down' to an angry woman. All he could do now was duck, and hope she didn't start chucking his shoes. But she had dissolved into tears instead, and now sank down on the floor, a wailing ball of misery.

Ben put his arms around her, safely from behind, and hung on until the storm of weeping had passed and she had stopped trying to twist around and hit him. He rested his chin on her shoulder and spoke softly.

'Now, are you gonna tell me what this is about? Hmm? Because I'm at a loss, Tammy. You haven't been yourself for a while, and I understand that, but I've just come home to take you out for a nice lunch, and I find you crying and carrying on, I mean, what is it? Is it hormones?' Even as the words left his mouth, his brain was screaming in horror, trying to call them back. *You moron*, he raged at himself. *You know perfectly well never to say the 'H' word to a woman.* Tammy was staring at him, an expression of disgust and loathing on her face. He had only ever seen her look like that once before, and that had been when Tom had sicked up a furball in her moccasin, and she'd slid her bare foot into it.

'Look,' he went on, in tones that he hoped were both soothing and persuasive, 'any chance we can sit down and talk about this, maybe over lunch?'

## ❧CHAPTER TWELVE☙

Tammy stared at her ex-boyfriend. She couldn't believe him. He was just like Neville after all. Men were all the same, she supposed. More than anything, she felt utterly humiliated, remembering her thoughts of the morning. She had been so close – this close – to reversing her decision to break up with him, and all the time he'd been laughing up his sleeve, screwing around with God knew who. The paper had been quite explicit, the list of entries excruciatingly detailed. It was a list of women's names, with their addresses and telephone numbers, their marital status, for God's sake, and a notes section beside each one. 'Likes it up the arse,' said one entry. 'Three way, either sex,' said another. He wasn't just a lying, cheating arsehole – he was a pervert. And he wanted her to go for lunch, as if nothing had happened, as if he'd just come home on a normal day and she'd been at her desk, working... part of her yearned so strongly to go back to that normality, even if it had been all lies, that she actually found herself leaning sideways.

'No, Ben,' she choked out, biting off each word as if it had personally insulted her. 'I don't want to have lunch with you. I don't even want to see you, ever again.' She delivered a vicious kick to the box at her feet. 'So just take all your shit and get out of my house.'

'What – what the – Tammy, what's happened?'

Look at him, acting all innocent. Just so had Neville looked when she had walked in on him – although his pants round his ankles and her friend spreadeagled on the kitchen table had prevented it from being as convincing as it might otherwise have been. But they were all the same. Men. Bastards.

'This!' She snatched the incriminating paper from where it still lay on the floor by their bed and threw it in his face. It didn't really throw well; she should have crumpled it up again, she thought. Preferably with a rock inside. 'This happened! You cheating, lying fucker!'

Ben stooped to pick up the paper. 'What's this?' He stared at it in incomprehension as she stood, heaving with righteous wrath. 'Catherine... married... likes it up the – good Lord! What is this? Theresa... married... wants to be punished... where did you find this?'

'It was in your stuff, Ben, that you emptied out of your pocket. Your lying, cheating, filthy pocket. This list of perverts. Adulterous perverts. You bastard. I thought you were different, you're all the same, lying bastards...' She punctuated her words with whacks about the head from the handful of shirts she was holding. 'I hate you!'

Unforgivably, Ben had started laughing. More than laughing – he was dancing about even as he shielded his head from the stinging whacks she was delivering. 'You cracked it!' he hooted. He seized her in a hug and showered kisses all over her face. 'My clever girlfriend!'

Tammy struggled, even as she longed to subside into his arms. Her nose was full of the warm, familiar smell of him, with just a hint of lemon... 'Get off me, you pervert bastard.'

'Tammy, listen, don't you realise what this is?'

'Gee, lemme think. Could it be... a printout from your little black book? You filthy (whack) pervert (whack) bastard? (whack whack whack).'

Ben stood, shielding his face with his arms, shaking with silent laughter. Somehow, it just wasn't the response she'd been aiming for. She had been more shooting for abject sorrow and shame. Perhaps with a little genuine remorse in there. The strength drained out of her whacking arm. She felt very tired, tired and sad and drained. Her efforts at doing up her house suddenly seemed pointless and childish. What good was a layer of paint? The whole place was a dump.

Ben had taken her shoulders in his hands. 'Are you ready to listen? Come on, Tammy, rule of law, remember? We don't condemn people without a fair trial?'

Tammy's eyes were pricking and she could feel her nose starting to run. She was damned if she was going to start crying again. She sniffed, hard, prompting Ben to offer his handkerchief.

Don't look at me with that bloody fond smile, she wanted to scream. You fake bastard. But the words died in her throat. Was she being unfair? It wouldn't hurt, she supposed, to listen to his story. It would be good for a laugh, later on. *You're never going to laugh about this, you fool*, whispered a small voice in the back of her head. *He's the best man you've ever met, don't throw him away without giving him a chance. You'll feel better about yourself later,* the voice continued, *if you know you've been fair.*

She looked at the man in front of her, flat abs, chiselled features with just a hint of softness about the lips, and that one errant lock of wavy hair falling over his forehead. She sighed. He was perfect. She looked back at her memories. The big heart, the great sense of humour, the thoughtfulness. The reliability. When, she asked herself, had he ever lied, to her or to anybody? When had he ever been late without calling, or failed to do something he'd said he'd do? *Give him a chance,* urged the voice. *You won't find another one like this one.*

She let out a long breath she hadn't realised she'd been holding. 'Alright, then. What is that paper?' Turning, she led the way to the kitchen. All serious talks had to take place at the kitchen table. It was how she'd been brought up.

***

Ben chuckled as he followed Tammy to the kitchen. How she would laugh when she knew it all. He quickly wiped the grin off his face as she turned. Never laugh in the presence of an angry woman. It had been advice his father had given him when he'd been sixteen, and it had never steered him wrong. However much a woman liked to laugh, they were as sensitive as cats if they thought anyone might be laughing at them. Ben didn't think it was manipulative to hide his laughter. It was, to him, a matter of courtesy.

He filled the kettle and put it on to boil. Of course they'd have tea. You needed tea for any kind of serious talk in the home. This was something his mother had taught him. Ben had grown up in a happy home, and had stored away all of the advice he'd received from both his parents about how that kind of home was made and maintained. The small, familiar acts of brewing tea brought a comforting touch of normality to even the worst situation, and the few minutes it took provided a breathing space for everyone to calm down a bit.

She was still watching him with that hostile glare. Ben ignored it and got down her favourite mug, a big, lopsided affair in bright yellow that she'd bought at a school fête. He busied himself with making the tea, deliberately keeping his back to her, giving her a little bit of space and time to calm down. It worked much, much better than *telling* a person to calm down, which nearly always, in his experience, worked about like pouring petrol onto a fire. As a general duties cop he had often made use of this technique when faced with excited people, taking a few minutes to find a page in his notebook, or even stepping away and pretending to take a radio call. This had often resulted in situations resolving themselves without the need for an arrest. Therefore, he took his time, jiggling the teabags to make the tea good and strong. You could ruin a good cup of tea by taking out the bag too soon. Shielding the cups with his body, he added an extra spoonful of sugar to Tammy's. Whatever had got her so upset was, he reasoned, in the same class as shock, and therefore the extra bit of sugar would do her good.

'Right,' he began, sliding the mugs onto the table. 'That paper. You want to know where that came from, am I right?' He felt the grin of triumph rising to his face again at the thought of his case, his miraculously solved case, and fought it down, forcing his face into an expression that he hoped was appropriately sober and respectful. Tammy had folded her arms and was looking at him with a 'go on, excuse boy, I can use a good laugh' expression.

'I didn't tell you what Tom was doing in Don Blackman's office,' he began. 'Thing is, he'd knocked over the wastepaper basket and he was playing with a bit of screwed-up paper, you know how he does.'

This met with a grudging nod, although her eyes had gone even more slitty.

'Well, see, Blackman was right behind me, and I didn't want him yelling that Tom'd made a mess, so when I picked him up I just grabbed the paper he was playing with and quickly shoved it in my pocket. So he didn't see, right?'

Another nod, a raised eyebrow.

'This paper, Tammy. Now, I'll have to check it, but I reckon these women are all clients of Yarralove. If they are, this'll be enough to get a warrant. We can seize his computer, and with any luck, there'll be all the evidence we need to hang the fucker out to dry.'

Good, she'd unfolded her arms and was reaching for the paper.

'You mean... this is evidence?'

'You bet it's evidence. It's enough to ground a reasonable suspicion that he's involved in the hack. If these women are all on the Yarralove database, and I wouldn't mind betting on that.'

'Well, what are you waiting for? We can hop online right now and check it!' She was already up and out of her chair, heading for the bedroom, her eyes sparkling. 'Come on! There's no time to lose!'

Ben cleared his throat. 'Ah-hem. Come on back, mate, we haven't finished our talk. About Us. A minute ago, you were stuffing my clean shirts in a box and kicking me out of the house. And committing assault, I might add, which is an indictable offence.'

She froze in the doorway, excitement dropping away almost visibly. Her shoulders drooped. She looked as if she might start crying again.

'Oh, Ben. I'm so sorry – I thought – I just – oh, God, I'm so, so sorry.'

'Come on back and sit down, Tammy. We need to clear this up for good. I don't want you jumping up and down and throwing me out in the street every time something triggers off a memory about your loser ex.'

'Ben, I –'

'Come on.' He patted the table. 'Come and sit back down. 'It's okay. Tammy, it's okay. Come on.'

She resumed her seat, looking as if she thought she was about to be shot.

'Look, it's just that I – I need you to trust me, Tammy. I need to know you're not always going to be looking for something to suspect me of, alright? I've never given you any reason –  and this job, it's tough, sometimes. You know I pull the late nights, and sometimes I'll be gone all night, and I don't want to be always wondering if you think I'm off with some floozy. I don't want you to be always worrying, either. You can't live like that.'

'I know, Ben, I'm sorry – it's just that – Neville...'

'Yeah, well I'm not him, Tammy. I'm not like him, and it hurts me when you think I am. Look, I have never, not since I met you, I have never looked at anyone else. There hasn't *been* anyone else. Can't you understand that? You don't need to worry. I'm a one-woman man.'

She was crying again, crying hard. Ben didn't know what he'd said. He reached for her hand.

'Come on, Tammy. Stop that. You're crying about nothing.'

A watery smile broke through the tears. She wiped her nose on her sleeve. 'You're not leaving me?'

He snorted. 'Don't be daft. Where else would I find a woman with snot all over her sleeve? You dag. Besides, what about the baby? You think I'm letting my son or daughter grow up without a father?'

There was a shocked silence.

'What baby?'

There was another shocked silence. Then they both spoke at once.

'You mean – you're not –'

'Oh my God, you were only staying because you thought I was –'

'–pregnant,' they both finished together.

***

It was a long time before Ben and Tammy made it as far as Tammy's computer, a time during which little was said after the first shocked exclamations. Ben, horrified at the new trouble he had wrought, stammered out denials and reassurances, and then reverted to non-verbal reassurance, which took some time and necessitated an abrupt change of venue to the bedroom; this change of venue, however, did not involve going anywhere near the computer. It was some time before Tammy spoke again. When she did, it was in small, quiet murmurs, and had nothing to do with babies.

# CHAPTER THIRTEEN

B lackman had enjoyed his day. He had had two meetings with new divorce clients, both of them matters triggered by the revelations of his godhateswhores.com website. He'd called the council about that dog that kept shitting on his lawn, and had watched with pleasure as the ranger's van drove slowly down the street. He'd given Shelley an enormous bollocking for leaving the office window open, allowing that bloody cat to get in, which had to have happened on Friday as he'd found the window open on Saturday morning and had closed and locked it, and had made her get down on her knees and scrub the office kitchen floor, where the cat had not only pissed and shat, but also vomited. While she was scrubbing and sniffling, he had also yelled at her for not emptying his wastepaper basket, ignoring the fact he had forbidden her to enter his office while 'sensitive files' were being worked on. He'd given the teacher woman's wrongful dismissal file to the new kid to research, and had watched with pleasure as he struggled to get a grip on it. He'd yelled at him for chatting with Shelley. He'd had a fine lunch at the Commercial Club with his mates, and was comfortably full of Tournedos Rossini and Cabernet Sauvignon. Now, he was putting the finishing touches to a vicious rant about whoredom and idolatry, naming several of Yarrangong's prominent citizens and revealing the dubious sexual proclivities of a couple more. He chuckled fatly as he scanned his document for proofing errors. Pity he couldn't get Shelley to do this. It would be fun to watch her get all embarrassed.

There was a timid tap, and his door opened a few inches. He could see the stupid girl peering around the edge, as if she thought he was going to throw something at her. He glared at her, and snatched up a paperweight, just to see her flinch. Stupid little bitch.

'What the fuck is it, Shelley, I told you I wasn't to be disturbed.'

'There are two gentlemen to see you, Mr Blackman.'

'Bullshit,' roared Blackman. 'I didn't schedule

any appointments. Shelley, get in here! Did you make an appointment and not write it in my book? Well, did you?'

Her knees were shaking. Good.

'Answer me, Shelley, don't stand there looking stupid.'

She mumbled something he couldn't make out.

'Speak up, for God's sake!'

'Okay, Miss Winters, we'll take it from here, thanks.' The young man pushing his way into the room looked oddly familiar, although Blackman didn't recognise him. Cheap suit, polyester tie, a nobody. Blackman rose up to smite him, but his words died in his throat as the man pulled out a badge.

'Detective constable Ben Jackson. You are Donald Anthony Blackman?'

Blackman found his voice. 'I am, what the hell is this?'

'Mr Blackman, I have a warrant here to seize any and all computer devices, digital storage devices and digital media, and all files opened within the last thirty days. Can you step away from the desk, please. Okay, Macka, come on through.'

The door opened more widely, to admit a large, red-headed man carrying some device which, as he set it down and unfolded it, turned out to be a collapsible trolley. Blackman watched, his mind somehow both numb and spinning in tiny circles, as his computer was loaded onto the trolley and his desk searched. They were very efficient, he noted. The search of his office was all over in twenty minutes. Efficient, but they left a hell of a mess, pulling out all the law books from the big bookcase and dumping them on the floor in random piles. The complete set of Commonwealth Law Reports just about filled the floor, leaving a narrow walkway through which they presently guided the trolley. Blackman followed them out to the reception area, where Shelley and the new kid stood in a nervous huddle by the door. There were two uniformed cops out here, loading Shelley's computer onto another trolley. All his files were out of the cabinets and strewn about the place. All of the new files, he saw with a sinking sensation, were on the trolley with the computer.

'What's this?' he blustered. 'You can't go interfering with those files. That's client confidential material.'

'Sorry, sir, you can apply to the court. You right, guys? Thanks for your time, Mr Blackman. Sorry about the mess.'

Cheeky young blighter. Sorry about the mess, indeed.

Blackman had spent half an hour relieving his feelings by yelling at Shelley and the new kid before he remembered what he'd been working on when the police had arrived.

*****

'Tammy! You'll never guess what!'

Tammy freed her elbow with some difficulty and looked up at her friend. Andy was barely recognisable from the previous week. Gone were the tea-cosy hat and the dreadlocks, all shorn away into a sharp, modern cut. The layers of ethnic shirts and saggy-bottomed trousers had been replaced by sharply creased khaki pants, a v-neck sweater over a business shirt and tie, and polished loafers.

'Wow, Andy, you look great! How's the new job?'

'Oh my God, it's awesome! First day was a bit rough, old Blackman likes to do a bit of bullying, he's a bit of a prick actually, but my God, today! You'll never guess! We got raided! By the police! It was beyond awesome. Oh my God, I can't wait to get to work tomorrow!'

***

On Wednesday, Ben came home late and looking ragged, laden with an enormous bunch of yellow roses and a basket of gourmet cat treats. He sagged on the sofa as Tammy fussed around him, simultaneously trying to arrange the flowers in her one vase, which wasn't really big enough, ply him with tea and chocolate biscuits, and massage his shoulders.

Ben took a long sip of tea and propped his feet on the coffee table. 'Ahh, that hits the spot. It's been a hell of a day.'

Tammy settled on the sofa beside him, biting her lips to keep from pestering. Let him tell it in his own time. Tom hopped up and stretched out between them, exposing his long, white stomach for rubbing. The diamond collar twinkled and sparkled against his black fur.

'It's all there, Tammy. I'm still going through stuff, but we've definitely got him on the hack. He was working on a new piece when we seized the computer. He was actually in the document. Stupid bastard had everything in a folder called godhateswhores. Talk about careless! Thinks he's above the law, I suppose. He was down the station today, throwing his weight around and yelling. Janey was on desk, she got rid of him by threatening to book him for creating a disturbance in a public place.'

He set down his mug and stretched his arms above his head. Tammy could almost hear the crack of released tension.

'And you, you little monster. Tell you what, Tammy, Tom's the real hero of this operation. If he hadn't got himself locked up in that office – well, I never would have suspected Don Blackman, that's for sure. Never in a million years.'

'What'll happen to him?'

'Depends if we get convictions for everything, but besides the hacking charge, the OPP reckon we can get him on Obtaining a Financial Advantage by Deception.'

Tammy snorted. 'That doesn't sound like much.'

'Not much? Hey, that's Fraud. That's what the charge is called. Obtaining a Financial Advantage by Deception. One count of fraud for every file he's opened up that resulted from his hacking actions. He'll get slotted for sure.'

'Slotted. Hmmph.'

'Yeah, for a few years I reckon. Oh, and struck

off, of course. A fraud conviction, well it doesn't get much worse than that for a lawyer. Unless it's multiple fraud convictions. Heh heh. Couldn't happen to a nicer guy.'

'You really don't like him, do you? Apart from being a crook.'

'Well, put it this way, he's not the first person I think of when I'm making up my Christmas list. God, you should have heard him getting stuck into his poor little secretary when we were coming up the path, you could hear it right out in the street. Anyway,' he went on, moving Tom to the other side of the sofa, 'I reckon we have more important things to discuss, Ms Norman.'

***

It had all turned out for the best, Tammy told herself, switching off the sander and arching her back. The belt sander was hell to use, but she was determined to do it herself. After weeks of searching online, she'd finally found a product that would do the bedroom floor white – not pure white like the walls, but very pale, anyway. She imagined how the room would look, with furniture and curtains. Soft, gauzy white curtains, drifting in a warm breeze. All white on the bed, of course. And that bed... a queen size, she reckoned. Big enough to fit a tired cop and a small black cat. Tom would provide just the right note of contrast in the white room.

Those tortured weeks when she'd planned to break up with Ben seemed very far away now. How could she have been so stupid? She could only put it down to some kind of hormonal upset. Or a virus, perhaps. She sighed, thinking how hard she must have been to live with. But it was all in the past now.

Tom, hearing the quiet, came winding into the room, his tail waving in graceful question marks above his back, his mouth opening in a silent mew.

'Whattya reckon, Tom? Look good?'

It would do, he seemed to say. He jumped onto her lap and stood up, rubbing his face against her nose, the diamond collar scratching her chin.

'It'll do, I reckon,' said Tammy. 'For now.'

## THE END

# Also by Tabitha Ormiston-Smith

## NOVELS

**Dance of Chaos:** Lazy, frivolous, conceited and totally self-centred, Fiona MacDougall is not an asset to the workforce. When she applies for a transfer to the Infotech department of her company, she does so only in order to get an afternoon off work.

Can she succeed in her challenging new job?

Can she save her little brother from the consequences of his evil deeds?

Will Moses do something embarrassing to the vicar's leg again?

**Gift of Continence:** With the perfect wedding dress, what can go wrong? A great deal, as Fiona McDougall rapidly discovers. From the wedding from hell onwards, Fiona successively discovers that her new husband is stingy, bad-tempered and an adulterer.

**Where The Heart Is:** Widowed, broke and unemployed, Fiona moves to the country to save money. But she is not prepared for the realities of country life…or for whom she will meet.

**King's Ransom:** What really went on back in 1193? Was Richard Lionheart really the hero we think? Was John really that bad? And who was Robin Hood, no really, who was he?

**The Secret Summer of Peter Fotheringay:** Left at boarding school over the Christmas holidays, Peter expects to have a boring time. But when he goes exploring in the school's disused attic, he finds something that will change his world forever.

## COLLECTION

**Once Upon A Dragon:** Collected short fiction. A non-themed, cross-genre collection of short fiction, including fantasy, science fiction and horror as well as general fiction.

## NOVELLAS

**No Such Thing**: Twelve-year-old Callie has taken on the responsibility of running the house and looking after her father, following her parents' divorce. When the bank threatens to foreclose on their home, Callie is forced to admit that this is a problem even she can't solve, until help comes from an unexpected quarter. But Callie learns that all actions have consequences, and sometimes the price for getting what you want can be too high...

**Melanie's Diary:** Melanie's life is out of

control. Her status-hungry parents have forced her grandmother into a home, and she's under siege from the school bully. But things are going to get a lot worse before they get better...

**Dancing Feet:** Ashley is devastated when her widowed father returns from his business trip with a new wife and her two daughters in tow. Pushed to one side by the interlopers, can she make a new life for herself?

**Operation Tomcat (Operation Tomcat Book 1):** Left almost penniless after divorcing her cheating husband, Tammy moves to the country to reinvent her life. But life in a country town isn't as simple as it looks...

**Operation Camilla (Operation Tomcat Book 2):** A sleazy solicitor hacks into a dating website in order to boost his failing family law practice. But he doesn't count on Tom...

**Operation Badger (Operation Tomcat Book 3):** Detective Senior Constable Ben Jackson is handsome, kind, hard-working and diligent. He's also as thick as two planks.

Tammy Norman is clever as all get-out. She's also sillier than a wet hen.

And then there is Tom.

Tom is a cat.

**NON-FICTION**

**Grammar Without Tears:** This short collection of dialogues will solve the most frequently experienced problems of the grammatically challenged.

**Fifty Shades of Grammar:** Everyone, it's said, has one book inside him, but getting it out can be problematical. Perhaps you can't English very well, or you work long hours and just don't have time, or you started writing and then got stuck? Fear not, for help is at hand.

Packed with friendly, no-nonsense advice, Fifty Shades of Grammar will answer all those questions you were too afraid to ask. From sentence structure to punctuation, from setting up your workspace to support your efforts to overcoming the dreaded 'writer's block', from traps and pitfalls to avoid to editing, the problems faced by the novice writer are clearly addressed – and with LOLCATS!

With this book at your side, the only variables will be your talent and your commitment.